Alignment

Alignment

Written by Ina Dey

Chapter One

My eyes flutter open as the bright sunlight dances around the edges of my blinds, causing the throbbing pain I recognize all too well as the repercussions to my latest night out. My mouth was begging for liquid, not caring if it was alcoholic or not because of how dry it was. But my brain and liver were hoping for water. I roll over facing the window, figuring I might as well deal with the demons that are sure to haunt me the rest of the day.

DING.

My phone vibrates once and bleeds a long, loud alert piercing my ears, signaling someone needs to get ahold of me for whatever reason.

"what in the hell even happened??"

The message on my phone practically screams at me as though the sender is shouting at me in real time. *What the hell even did happen last night?* The latest night out runs through my head. Obviously missing some major events. Indulging in too much damn alcohol will do that.

I'm certain the pairing of weed probably didn't help my missing memory. But what I do remember was nothing shy of… *interesting* to say the least.

To start the day yesterday, I rolled out of bed around two in the afternoon. Which has become the norm since summer break began, I mean, what else would a college student who was living with her aunt in the sunny state of California do? After slumping out of my bed and dragging my feet to my bathroom, I stepped into the shower. Letting the scorching hot water run through my hair and down my back always helped to wash away the alcohol-induced migraine. I will surely do the same today.

After surviving my shower and texting my friends to make a plan, I return to my room and pick out my clothes.

I decide on a pair of light-washed denim shorts and a deep, forest green tank top that shows a decent amount of bust and a sliver of my abdomen. Hardly allowing my belly-button piercing, that I've had since I was 16, to peek out. I apply the light amount of makeup I always wore. Some concealer desperately needed for the bags under my eyes, filling in my eyebrows, teasing my eyelids with a nude-shade of sparkle eyeshadow, and coating my eyelashes with mascara. I curled my hair allowing the long, thick, blonde strands to drape down my back with beach-wave style curls. My hair was easily my favorite feature, although some said it should be my forest green eyes, which is probably why that was my preferred color to wear. I needed to stand out in some way, given I missed most of the normal affection offered in childhood. The look was finished with my trusty black hightop Converse, my signature shoes.

As I was walking out my front door, turning the key to lock it, my phone sent me another alerting sound, *jeez I have got to change that tone*, dropping my keys to the ground. I grunted as I bent down to grab them, simultaneously reaching for my phone from my back pocket.

"see you at Blazer's?" The text came through from my best friend, Janet.

"that's the plan, stan" I replied.

On the drive to Blazer's, I thought about what the plan would be for the rest of the day and into night. As always, it probably would include drinking far too much, taking pictures to keep as no one would remember the little moments, and spending time with the group I was inseparable from.

Once I pull my old, beat up, dark blue Toyota into the small parking lot of Blazer's, I take a moment to admire the building that has become the friend group's go-to place.

It looks like an old, decrepit building from the outside. With its peeling dark red paint and lopsided signs. Yet when you walk through the doors into the air conditioned building, you see the lively atmosphere it holds. The walls are lined with LED beer signs, posters, and typical bar games. What made this place different to us, rather than it being close enough to every one of my friends, is that it had the ambiance we adored. Lighting that was a yellow-orange hue rather than booming white, an outdoor patio with plenty of tables to hold a few large groups or several small ones, and music that just simply brought happiness with a jukebox option to play almost any song the patrons wanted.

When I get out of my car, I see my friends standing around Janet's car across the parking lot. Max, Lily, and Korey all turn around once Janet spots me and waves, causing Lily to run towards me and the rest to follow. I hadn't seen Lily in a few days since she disappeared, odd because the group gets together every day. She never explained it, but my guess is she ran out of her medication. Again.

"Oh my *godddd*" Lily sings. "How are you Brooke? I feel like it's been *weeks* since I saw you last! God your hair looks incredible! New shampoo?"

"Lily! Oh I missed you!" I say as I give her a big hug, "Stop disappearing like that and it won't feel like weeks!" I sense I struck a slight nerve.

"Well that's what happens when the doc wants to see you before renewing your shit even though the diagnosis hasn't changed!" She said with a dragged out tone of sarcasm.

"I get it, but I am glad to see you!"

The rest of the group says their hello's and we begin walking towards the door of Blazer's.

Once inside our home-away-from-home, we step up to the bar and order our drinks with Tilly, our favorite bartender. And not only because she over-pours our liquid courage.

I order my signature Honey Trap while everyone else orders their favorites. Max demands we all take shots to get our day truly started, even though it's only four o'clock. There is no argument and we all grab our shot glasses full of bottom-shelf Tequila with a rim of salt.

We hold up our glasses as Korey shouts "For summer!" Everyone licks their salt, shoots their Tequila, and bites into their limes.

The saltiness prepares my taste buds for the burning poison which I can feel all the way to my toes. Awakening my stomach just enough before the lime helps my system settle. There is something about biting into lime that gives me so much happiness. *Or maybe that's the Tequila I just threw back.*

We grab our mixed drinks and head towards our favorite table, in the corner closest to the games and a perfect view of the front door. With billiards on our left and darts on our right, we split into groups to tackle the fun that is waiting to be had in simple bar games.

After quite a few drinks, lots of games, some greasy yet delicious bar food, and a shit ton of laughs, we finally

5

decide to step outside onto the patio we loved so much. When we walked through the door, we find some of the other regulars we frequently see here, and say our hello's as we pass by them to our favorite round table. Once again in the corner with a view of the door. Janet sits next to Max, his hand around her waist, Lily next to me as we sit somewhat across from the lovebirds, and Korey sitting between the two groups on my right.

The only thing I didn't like about the patio was that there was only one entrance, also serving as the exit. I have a thing with corners and doors apparently. My therapist used to say that it was normal to have some fear about needing an exit plan given what's happened in my past. As much as it makes sense, it fucking *sucks*.

That was another reason I saw my friends day in and day out, they helped me stay much more grounded than I would be on my own. Guardian angels if you will. Janet, being my life-long best friend who was nothing shy of gorgeous, always had a way to cheer me up. Even in the midst of a breakdown.

"So what kind of trouble are we getting into tonight, ladies and gents?" Max asks the group with a devious smirk on his face.

He and Janet had been together for as long as I could remember, that being only about two years. My memory is shot from the weed and booze I hide my fears and hurt behind. What can I say?

"I was thinking we could swing by Ashton's place, heard he's throwing one of his famous Thursday night bashes?" Lily responds, begging for approval.

"Ashton's? Girl we all know you're in love with him just admit it to yourself already" I reply, giving her a daring look and lightly shoving her shoulder with the hand not occupied by my fourth Honey Trap.

"Oh please, he's still head-over-heels with that girl from Colorado, whatever her fucking name was." Lily never liked her. Luckily she wasn't around for long.

"Well, with no other ideas, I say we fuck it up at Ashton's" Max declares, giving Lily a look with more meaning to the statement 'fuck it up'.

We all sigh in passive agreement as we finish our drinks and stand up, heading back inside to say goodbye to Tilly and close our tabs. Approaching the bar, Janet and I begin to stumble over our feet just a little. Not enough to look overly intoxicated to the strangers around us, but enough that our closest friends can tell we aren't sober. Janet and I were always the ones to feel drunk the fastest, but we kept trucking along for the hell of it.

When we got to the bar, Janet pulled on my arm, slightly slurring her words with the scent of Tequila coming out along with "Don't look, but he's here." My skin instantly gets hot and I know who she is talking about without even a second thought.

Chapter Two

10 years prior

It's my 15th birthday. Birthdays have never been some big fiasco like they are for most families. I guess you could say that's because I come from a broken family. Like, *really* broken.

My mom died when I was three years old. Still a new life in this world. My dad was arrested long before that, when I was around one as the story goes. Because of that, I was dragged to live with my aunt and uncle in their always-too-hot California home. Originally, though, I'm from the cold, harsh state of Maine. Where winters were brutal and summers were mildly enjoyable but beautiful none-the-less.

After moving in with my aunt and uncle, things were less than great. My aunt was a raging alcoholic bitch. Whereas my uncle was a little too comfortable with the idea of a three year old running around the house.

At first though, it was decent. Ice cream whenever I wanted, staying up late to cuddle on the couch, things like that. But as time went on, oh boy did things change. My uncle became abusive. Not in the hitting and yelling kind of way. But the way that makes a child either hypersexual or less-than-interested in the future. It started light, getting more intense and agonizing as he became more confident.

Because my aunt struggled with substance abuse, or should I say addiction, she was never around emotionally to lend an ear, or provide an escape for that matter. I was never able to stand up for myself when things were happening that I knew deep down were criminal.

This birthday though, I finally wanted to change that. I woke up prepared to run away and make a better life for myself, only 15 years into it.

That was a short-lived dream however because when I did finally wake up ready for the day, there was pounding on the door. Confused, I headed towards it, wondering who the hell would be assaulting our front door so early on a Wednesday morning. On my way there, my aunt stopped me, sober for one of the only times I remember seeing since I was seven. Only because that's as far as my memory reaches.

"Go wait in your room. It's too early for this," she spits with anger in her voice because she hadn't yet calmed herself with alcohol.

I walk down the hall, stopping just out of sight but with ears to hear. The front door opens with that usual creak of the hinges I have grown accustomed to over the recent years.

"Can I help yo... HEY! What the hell?"

Suddenly, five decorated men in uniforms are rushing through the living room, practically trampling over top of me to reach my aunt and uncle's room.

"DON BARING, COME OUT OF THE ROOM SLOWLY, WITH YOUR ARMS IN THE AIR!" The police shout with an obvious tactical formation as they filled the hallway in front of the bedroom door.

"Beverly, what's happening?" I cry to my aunt, scared of the answer. Hell, scared of everything happening in front of my eyes.

"I said go to your damn room, Brooklyn!" she shouts back at me.

With that, I silently run to my bedroom at the other end of the hallway, leaving the commotion as I wrap my brain around why the police are here. Suddenly it hits me.

Sitting in the nurse's office at school, I try to come up with a lie about where the bruises came from.

"Brooklyn, I have to ask again. The P.E. teacher noticed bruises on your thighs. Do you remember how you got them?" She asks me with kind eyes and open ears, hoping I'll give her the truth. But I could never do that. Still, 12 years after the abuse began, I couldn't open my mouth to reveal the torture I'd endured out loud.

"I fell off my bike on the way to school." I lied, the anxiety trying to escape through my shaking leg. "It was a whole big thing, you should've seen it." I chuckle, trying to shrug off the severity of her accusations.

"Brooklyn, your paperwork says you take the bus, not that you ride your bike." She takes a breath, holding my file in her hands. "I understand there are things that may happen behind closed doors that are hard to explain, but I need you to be honest with me."

I don't say anything, avoiding her sorrowful eyes filled with pain from imagining what *does* in fact happen behind closed doors.

She reaches across her desk and touches my shoulder lightly to focus my attention back on her and I back away with such great force I almost fall backwards from the chair I was sitting on. I straighten myself in the chair as she looks at me.

"Okay, well maybe your family just forgot to update the system when you started riding your bike to school, does that sound like a possibility?" She changes her tone, sounding more matter-of-fact. I look at her with tears beginning to pool in my eyes from the flashbacks her touch caused. *Damn I was fucked up.*

"Yeah that must be it." I summoned the courage to reply, ashamed of myself for not having the strength to come clean. I stand to leave her office and return to class. Grabbing my emerald backpack, turning to her one more time. She doesn't see me turn around, but I watch her grab the phone in her office and begin dialing a number. I knew then, she was too smart to believe my bluff.

Hearing the shouting from Don suddenly throws my head back to current times. After his screaming about something I can't quite make out, I hear one of the uniformed men speak.

"Don Baring, you have the right to remain silent. Anything you say can and will be used against you in a court of law. You have the right to an attorney. If you cannot afford an attorney, one will be provided fo…"

Their voices fade through the front door, Don being led out of the house. His face is red and his hands are linked behind him. A few minutes later I exit my room, cautiously, afraid of what I might see. As I walk through my door and down the hall, I see my aunt leaning against the pressed wood countertop in the kitchen, throwing back her liquid poison. *She doesn't miss a beat.* I carefully walk up to her, uneasy about her current mood, uncomfortable with the newfound silence.

She turns to look at me, drunkenness already beginning to take over her eyes. "You.. *You* are the reason my husband is gone! You are the reason for our life getting turned upside down! You are the reason I will *never* be happy again!" She screams at me, tears in her eyes and liquor in her words, pointing an accusatory finger.

I stop in my tracks, staring her down. She softens her gaze at me, seeming almost apologetic. I hesitate, as violent mood swings were common for her in this state of drunk, before she gets sleepy enough to fall asleep in any position known to man due to the intoxicating amount of booze in her system.

"What's going on?" I ask, worried about the outcome.

She looks at me, with the burning rage once again. "You got my fucking husband *arrested* that's what happened. You and your stupid fucking lies. Always wanting to be the center of attention no matter who it hurts around you."

Those words stung, because I have felt so neglected and unloved since the abuse started all those years ago. I look at her, astounded she thinks I'm always trying to be the center of attention. When in reality, I do everything I can to be nonexistent when I'm home. Scared my movements will make Don want to use me again.

"*Me?* How? I do nothing in this house except sit in my fucking room all day hoping your sick and twisted husband won't grab me by the feet when I'm sleeping and have his way with me!" The words pour out of my mouth before I'm even able to register what I'm saying.

"Do *not* use that tone with me." Her glare hammers into my soul. My heart is pounding in my ears so loud I can barely hear her response. I'm afraid she may finally break and throw her now-empty bottle straight at my head, leaving me with more bruises than I already have. "I will not sit here

13

and allow you to lie about Don hurting you!" Her fists are tight with fury.

My emotions have been bottled up for so many years I am not sure what is about to come out of my mouth. But I know something is about to erupt inside of me and the shrapnel will be felt by others.

"*Lie*?" I yell back with every ounce of oxygen in my breath. "I have put up with Don's grimy shit since I was three years old!" I take a breath. "I'm sorry I never had the confidence to speak up about it but it's not my fault you've been too drunk to register any real thoughts or emotions since my mom died!" I continue to burrow down into her soul with my words, hoping just a few would stick. She looks at me, both of us full of rage.

"Do you not believe me? Here!" I shout, pulling my sweatpants down, exposing my boyshort underwear and tan legs covered in bruises, all of different stages of healing. Some green, some blue, some purple. Rolling my sleeves up to show her the scars where his teeth would pierce into my skin when he just couldn't help himself. Those scars are now beginning to fade because he recently stopped biting, knowing they were harder for me to hide from the world, trying to lessen the chance of being caught.

She stops, puts down her bottle, and walks over to me. Reaching out a hand, I back away, just as forcefully as I did backing away from the nurse. Though now, I wasn't sitting in a chair so I could actually break free.

She realizes what her attempted touch did to me and begins to examine my hurt from afar. Only a few feet, but close enough to see the damages written across my body.

"Could I make up these lies if I didn't have the proof to back them up, *Beverly*?" I say with the heaviest enraged tone I can muster.

Her eyes go soft, softer than I have ever seen in my 12 years of living here. She takes a large, painful breath, and looks at me, all of me. Her eyes turn soft and she seems *sorry*.

"Oh honey, I had no idea" She empathizes, seeming stone-cold sober.

And that made this the *best* and *worst* birthday ever.

Chapter Three

We successfully paid our tab with Tilly and walked out of the bar without incident. At this point, I was more on the sober side than the drunk side. The near-heart attack I experienced just moments before made my blood process the alcohol much quicker than I anticipated. Once we reach Janet's car, we group around as we always do.

"Who's driving to Ashton's?" Korey asks, wanting to continue the buzz he got from the drinks at Blazer's.

"I say we all meet up at our place and then just walk, it's not that far, right?" Max replies, offering to meet at his and Janet's apartment just down the street.

We lived in a relatively large city, but I guess it was a somewhat small portion of it, where we all are within 10 minutes of each other and the places we frequent.

I climb into my car, having Korey ride shotgun since he was tipsy and I was newly sober. On the way to Max and Janet's, Korey looks over at me with curiosity in his eyes. "So what were the red cheeks and huffing-puffing about at Blazer's?"

I focus on the road, knowing the drive is short and he wouldn't have much time to get all his questions in. "I just had a bout of anxiety and needed some fresh air," I reply while trying my best to sound honest.

"That's bullshit and you know it. I saw Janet grab ahold of you before your vibes changed. Come on Brookeyyy, we've known each other for ages." He pleas.

He's right, we have known each other for ages. The whole group came together as friends a few years after I was suddenly relocated to California. There were a few 'side characters' that came and went, but Korey, Lily, Max, Janet, and I were the crew that stayed together. No matter what. And they always looked out for me.

I look over at him, finally at the street light indicating the drive is almost over. "She told me he was there. I didn't want or need to look and I just had to get out of there."

"How is it that he gets you going like that and I can't?" He jokes. Korey was always making jokes about how he was *so* in love with me, but we all know he's the class clown of the group, as well as the fact that I'm not the only one he jokes like that with.

I laugh back at him, "You know I love you. Always have and always will, but you and I have friend-zoned each other. And it will forever stay that way" I flash him a friendly smile and blow him a sarcastic, dramatic kiss.

As everyone walks into Janet and Max's front door, Korey, Lily, Janet, and I take seats on the couch. Janet cues up our summer music playlist using the Alexa sitting on the T.V. stand across the room. Max pours shots for all of us in the kitchen, his unspoken duty every time the party travels here. He calls out for us and we join him in the kitchen.

We circle up around the island in the middle of the large room, grabbing our shot glasses. In unison we wet the web on our hands between our thumb and the back of our hand with our tongues, taking turns pouring salt to the wet spot, then we lick the salt off our hands, throw back our shots, and bite into our limes.

"Whew," Lily and Janet say after making sour faces at the spectrum of tastes that just flew through our mouths.

"God damn, always gives me the chills!" I state, giving a quick shimmy in an attempt to deter the goosebumps popping up throughout my body.

Janet grabs me by the arm once again and pulls me to her room, no one really noticing because they were deep in conversation about the plan for tonight.

As we walk into her room, sitting on her bed, she looks at me, the seriousness of her eyes make my stomach turn more than the liquid we just drank.

"So when did you talk to him last?" She asks, looking for my honest answer.

The way just the mention of *him*, name or not, can get my head spinning amazes me. I can't lie to Janet, I've never been able to. She knows all of my truths and troubles. She was the first one to notice the bruises and bite marks all those years ago, never threatening me or treating me differently because of the things I couldn't control. She confessed to me a few years back that she was part of the reason Don got arrested. Janet went to the school nurse, not the P.E. teacher, he didn't bat an eye.

I look at her with a smirk on my face, "At the party two weeks ago, we ended up in the bedroom upstairs for a while, which was almost magical…" I sigh, turning away, "… Until Cheryl walked in trying to find the bathroom she was one measly door away from." Janet sighs with me as I continue. "Then it just became really awkward because that was the first time we had really *tried* to try something, all the other times we saw each other was in passing or short bursts of flirtation." I shake my head, "Pretty sure he blocked my number that night."

She shakes her head with regret, "Girl, you know he thinks you're hot, there's no way he blocked you. I heard he'll be there tonight! Go for a redo!"

"If he didn't make my insides tingle at the thought of him then maybe I'd go for it. You know we've had this sort of back and forth thing going on for a while. As much as I crave his undivided attention, I know there's other girls that he wants to give it to more than me." I mutter the last sentence knowing Janet would have a counter.

19

"Bitch, stop. You deserve every ounce of attention Kasey has to offer as long as he deserves you in return. You are the greatest woman walking this earth and you know it." She gives me a hug as we stand, "And don't forget, your past doesn't define you."

Returning to the kitchen we find our friends in the same spot we left them in. Still talking about plans for tonight, but also talking about what happened the night before, the night before that, and so on and so on. Laughing overtakes the room, drowning out the background music.

We walk out of Max and Janet's once we were properly tipsy. We left Max and Janet's blissfully air conditioned apartment and were met with the evening sun beating down with low rays of heat. The sky was a broad spectrum of oranges and there was a slight cooling breeze from the ocean a few miles away. A typical summer night in our sweet town in California.

We walked the mile or so down the street, taking a few turns along the way. When we get a few houses away, we can hear the music seeping through the walls and the open door. A small crowd gathered at the bottom of the stairs. Walking through the door we are greeted by Ashton and a few others we are acquainted with.

"Hey guys! Long time no see! Glad you could make it!" He smiles at the five of us, giving extra attention to Lily. Ushering us to the fridge in the back of the house to grab a drink. We happily oblige, shuffling past groups of people scattered throughout the house, at least 50 bodies stacked inside with another 10 lingering outside.

In the kitchen I grab a bottle of Tequila and start the night off right taking a heavy pull from the glass half gallon. Max, Janet, Lily, and Korey follow suit, not caring how much we ingest because no one has to drive.

I take another pull before grabbing the first beer to find my hand, needing constant liquid courage before I inevitably run into Kasey. Lily comes up to me, putting an arm around my shoulder and dragging me to the living room while the rest of the group follows.

In the living room, there's LED beer signs on the beige walls just like the ones at Blazer's, banners and flags of different teams I've never heard of, and the smell of shitty piss-beer spilled on the sticky floors. My black high top Converse fighting slight adhesive trying to keep me in place.

We join another group of friends, their names I hardly remember because I was so intoxicated when I first 'met' them. Music blasts through the speakers, hardly allowing conversation to take place without trying to match the volume level.

"Did you see the way Ashton looked at you?" I yell-ask to Lily, hoping she noticed the look in his eyes as he talked to her when we arrived.

"What do you mean? He just said 'hi' to everyone." She shyly responds and I can see her cheeks gaining color.

"Wrong. He was looking you up and down and gave everyone else less than an ounce of attention, don't try to deny it."

She blushes at that comment, knowing full well what he was trying to accomplish with his additional glances. She's had the hots for Ashton since her scumbag boyfriend cheated on her last year, finally allowing herself to feel things again rather than constantly building walls up. Ashton has recently started playing into the passive flirting, now making Lily shy to respond.

I give her a look saying 'go to him' without needing to speak. She understands my eyes and turns to find him in the crowd leaning against a wall in the other room just as his gaze finds her. She looks back to me one more time as I brush the few loose strands of blonde hair out of her eyes, giving her the nod of approval. With that, she turns and heads in his direction.

I am left in my own company with a freshly finished drink. Needing something to cool down my nerves, I head towards the kitchen. As I pass through the noisy room full of swinging bottles and laughing peers, I see Kasey standing in the corner on his phone, not yet noticing I walked into the room.

My steps slow as I get closer to the fridge, ultimately closer to Kasey. His sky blue short sleeve shirt allows the scattered tattoos to escape into view of the naked eye. Tripping on my own feet brings his bright ocean eyes to focus on mine. My heart skips a beat. Several to be truthful. Realizing how his shirt brings out the color of his eyes while contrasting his dark brown, almost black curly hair, makes my skin hot like it's going to melt off of my body.

"Oh hey, Brooke." He pauses, scanning my body with his eyes. "How have you been?" He sounds excited, voice raspy, while also sounding hesitant.

"Not too bad, just trying to keep my head above water, you?" I reply timidly.

"Same old, same old." He slides his phone back into his front pocket, I focus on his hands and remember how soft they were the last time they trailed up my skin. "So," he continues, "Why haven't I heard from you since... Well, the last time we saw each other?"

"Oh, I have uh... I've been busy, you know, family stuff." I blurt out the last part of the sentence as quickly as it comes to mind, not wanting him to know I was too embarrassed to reach out, thinking he didn't want to hear from me anyway.

"I've heard you've been busy, but nothing about family stuff was mentioned." He calls out my bluff, giving me a look I can't quite decipher. A hint of worry with a side of curiosity, knowing that by 'busy' I mean partying.

I open the fridge and once again grab whatever beverage finds my hand first, cracking open the tab and taking a long drink, desperate for some mitigation of the awkwardness sure to follow.

"To be honest with you, Kasey..." my heart begins to beat faster. I'm not sure if it's because of the alcohol, the truth I'm about to spill, or his vibrant blue eyes staring into mine. At the same time I take a deep breath, the noise of the house suddenly ceases after tires screech, locking up. A loud, strident metal crash takes place outside.

Chapter Four

     Half of the crowd inside the house, including my closest friends, begin to shuffle outside and join those already grouped up just beyond the front door. We are silent as we look across the street at the fiery collision between a gold car and the thick trunk of a tree.

     "Oh *shit*." Ashton is the first to speak. "Does anyone know whose car that is?" Frantically pulling his cell phone out and dialing 911, explaining to the operator what just occurred with a sense of panic I have never seen from him.

Suddenly, someone from the outside party I don't entirely know, screams. Blood-curdling chimes fill the silence as she runs into the half-dead grass in front of the house, crossing the street as three others follow her. The people remaining in the house finally join everyone outside as mumbling begins to break the silence.

"What the *fuck* happened?"

"Who is that?"

"Isn't that Debbie's mom's car?"

"I thought it was Aaron's dad."

"Is that Charlotte?"

"Are they okay? That looks *bad*."

Overlapping chatter and dozens of questions later, sirens begin to quiet us down as they arrive with the red and white lights allowing us to see the carnage in waves.

Between the flashes of blinding light, we see two tires in the road, the front end of the vehicle crushed from making contact with another car parked on the street, and the rest of the crumbling car wrapped around the tree on the driver's side where it ended the out-of-control travels.

The fire department that responded uses their large engine to block the road from other traffic, as if there would be that many cars on the road at a quarter past midnight, as two men in heavy uniforms grab kits from the exterior doors of their truck. One gets out and puts wheel chocks under the rear tires, ensuring the engine doesn't grow a mind of its own, then joins the other two.

The two that grabbed kits quickly run to the gold car wrapped around the base of the evergreen, attempting to gain entry and question their newest patient.

The last to leave the engine begins walking up to us, an older man with salt and pepper hair, clean shaven, and tired eyes. Needing to talk to the potential witnesses, he asks who called it in.

"I called, but I'm not sure what happened." Ashton says with sadness in his voice, knowing the collision is most likely fatal. He has a history of losing people in accidents before and has a pretty good idea of what the outcome would be based on the mechanism of the crash.

They continue to talk about what happened, even though there wasn't much to be said. After a few moments, he excuses himself and goes to check in with the rest of his crew across the street at the scene of the accident.

No one can hear their conversations because of the constant rumbling coming from the engine blocking the roadway. Based on their slow actions lacking urgency, we know with just their body language the ramifications were in fact life-ending.

After 20 minutes of everyone standing around, unsure of what to do next, the original salt and pepper-haired fireman and a police officer walk up to Ashton. He freezes, his eyes unsure where to look, clearly as sober as the rest of us since the accident took place.

"Sir, I'd like to get an official statement from you as well as anyone else who might have seen something." The officer pulls out the notebook from his chest pocket, looking around at the lot of us.

"Well most of us were inside, but we heard it. Those guys were out here so they might be more helpful." Ashton points to the smaller group of people that were sitting around the patio before a life ended, two of the girls crying hysterically since realizing there was a fatality.

"Thank you, you guys take care now." He excuses himself to join those that were outside.

There are nine people that witnessed the crash, the girl that ran to the car and her three followers make up four of them. The one that ran is finally calming down as they all prepare to talk with the officer. My group listens from where we stand.

"I'm sorry you folks had to see this. These can be hard things to process so I want to make sure I remember to tell you all to reach out to someone if you need to. You don't need to go through all of these feelings alone." The group nods in agreement, anxious to hear what he says next.

"Can anyone explain to me what they remember?" He pauses, waiting for someone to speak up.

"We were all sitting around the patio, just having a good time. It's summer and we are on break from school you know? Sorry, anyway. We were hanging out and all of a sudden we heard screeching and looked up to the road." The storyteller takes a breath and dries the tears falling down his cheeks. "When we did we saw Charlotte's car hit a neighbor or someone parked on the street and then her car just completely lost control. It spun so many times and then slammed into that tree." He points at the large tree across the road with more tears forming in the corners of his eyes.

The officer writes down bullet points of the details he's receiving. Showing he is listening intently and not at all annoyed to be here, despite it being nearly one in the morning. "Okay, and then what did you guys do after the crash occurred?"

"A few of us ran over to check on her, she had just texted us that she was on her way from seeing a friend. She did tell us that she was drinking a little with that friend but we didn't think she meant *that* much." He spills all the truth, knowing Charlotte can't get in trouble for her dumb decisions anymore. "When we got to her car, we could barely see past the airbags. But we knew with the amount of blood splattered on the windows that it wasn't good."

There was faint crying from some girls we didn't know a few feet away from us as this detail was revealed.

Charlotte was a girl that we had grown up with, but from a distance. Never super close friends with our group but we knew each other in passing. Hearing her name as the one involved in the crash made my heart break for her family and closer friends.

Once the commotion settled down, a majority of the party attendees left, some opting to drive if they felt alright, some ordering Ubers or Lyfts to be extra cautious, and most walking the short distance to their homes. There were maybe 20 people left that wanted to either sober up in the safety of a home, or just relax and debrief with their closest friends.

There were four or five other people I recognized other than the usual four I spent all my time with that decided to stay. The rest were a mystery to me. A few went to the kitchen to talk amongst themselves, some went to a bedroom upstairs with the rightful resident of that room to hang around, and the remainder of us stayed on the couch. Lily, Max, Kasey, Janet, Korey, Ashton, two others I'm merely acquainted with, and I sit crammed onto the small sectional. Afraid to speak.

After a few minutes of loud silence, Korey grabs our attention away from the images in our mind of what occurred just an hour prior. "Just to break the ice, is everyone doing okay? That was some heavy shit."

One at a time we respond, timid and horror-struck.

"Wish I closed my eyes the moment I walked out the front door," Janet shakes her head. Max reaching over and putting his hand on her thigh to calm her down.

Ashton inhales deeply before speaking, "What just happened? She's really dead?"

"Where do we go from here?" Lily says with alcohol and panic.

I stay silent, the only thoughts running through my mind were reminders. A reminder that there was a large possibility that it could have been my aunt, not Charlotte, years ago before she finally agreed to go get treatment for her alcoholism. Reminders of why I need to keep my shit in check before I make a mistake like that. Reminders why I need to make sure my *friends* keep their shit in check before *they* make a mistake like that.

"She was such a sweet girl, she was struggling lately with drinking too much, I should have spoken up." One of the acquaintances, Robbie, says to no one in particular, staring at the ground with his head in his hands.

"That's not on you, who could you have gone to? We're adults now." Robbie's friend replies with sorrowful eyes.

We sit around and continue to talk for a while. Half of us are deep in thought and the other half contribute to the careful conversation taking place. Though we each have different responses, we are equally upset. Some of us are hiding it better than others. Thankfully, that was a specialty of mine. Bottling things up was something I learned to do at a very young age.

Eventually the mood lightens a little and we decide to part ways. Before standing with my guardian angels to leave, Kasey makes eye contact with me, silently begging me to stay behind and talk to him.

I tell Janet I will catch up with them later and they can head out, she protests. "Don't be silly Brooke, we'll wait out front for you. Take your time, babe." Giving me a much needed embrace, leaving the sweet smell of her shampoo behind, before departing out the door with the rest of my friends.

Kasey stands and holds his hand out to me, hesitantly I place my hand in his and let him lead me to the back yard.

Chapter Five

My heart is pounding so hard I'm worried the muscle will burst altogether. Morning runs have been helping me out a ton lately, almost as much as they hurt. Finishing my run a block down from where I live, I end the workout on my watch.

```
Workout Complete!
Summary:
4.2 miles
32 minutes
Average HR: 154 BPM
```

Not too bad of a run if you ask me. My favorite part of my morning runs are the last block I take at a slow pace. That's when my brain is able to start thinking again and I feel like I live at the top of the world. In reality, I live in a three bedroom condo-type building. Three floors with one bedroom on each floor. The bottom floor houses Arlo. The second floor has Charlie, a bathroom, and the kitchen. And I'm on the third floor, with my own bathroom. I was able to snag the best end of the stick because I am a full time student, after all, gotta have a good environment to study peacefully, right?

I kick off my shoes when I get inside, dropping my keys back into my pocket. Now the worst part of the workout, climbing two flights of stairs to get to my portion of the house.

My phone pings while I'm in the shower but the water feels so good. Rinsing the rest of the soap out of my hair, I wonder if I should rub one out real quick. I shake my head and think about this summer break instead. I only have two more semesters before I graduate my nursing program and then have to decide where I want to practice medicine. That's not an easy thing to think about and it consumes a good amount of my mind. But not as much as she does.

I get out of the shower and dry my hair using the towel and then wrap it around my waist and grab my phone.

"Party tonight? My house." Ashton had said.

"Yessir" I reply, locking my phone and setting it back on the counter. I walk into my bedroom and open my dresser drawer full of T-shirts. I grab a blue shirt with simple, scattered black ink lines across it in a random fashion, black jeans, and slip on my white AirForce shoes. I walk back into my bathroom and comb my hair out and then run my hands through it messily, checking that it's presentable. When I'm satisfied, I drop my phone into my front pocket.

It's already three o'clock and I haven't eaten anything. Walking downstairs, my roommate Charlie is sitting at the table eating a bagel.

"Can I swipe one of those?" I ask, nodding my head towards his plate.

"Yeah for sure." He says back, returning to his phone.

I grab a bagel, pop it in the toaster, and get out the cream cheese in preparation for the best breakfast of champs. Pouring myself a cup of coffee and sitting at the table, Charlie asks me "Hey, you talk to Brooke at all lately?"

My chest flutters, I can feel myself getting warmer, "No, why?" I answer, feeling almost defensive for some reason.

"Just curious." He takes the last bite of the bagel, "You going to Ashton's tonight? Supposed to be a good fucking time as always."

"I was thinking about it, yeah. Do you know who's going?"

33

"Nah, why? You hoping for someone certain?" He says, playfully poking fun at me.

"I'm chill." I laugh back and start to eat my breakfast bagel. I sit on the couch and turn on the TV. Flipping through show titles, struggling with what to watch, I finally turn on Storage Wars and start swiping through my phone. My thoughts can't seem to relax. I can't get her out of my head, in the best way possible. I've always been curious about what happened when we were younger, but I never got close enough to ask. Not that it matters too much, her past doesn't define her. Just like mine doesn't define me.

My mom wasn't the most active parent in my childhood. She actually caused a lot of problems in my life. But I think that she's part of the reason I chose the profession I did. I want to help people in her situation, keep them alive, and get them out of those lifestyles.

Heroin was her drug of choice. I could count on one hand how many times I saw her sober since I turned 12. Four overdoses needing hospitalization since I was 16. I'm honestly not sure how she managed to keep custody of me, although it was probably because my father was in the picture. Even if he was emotionally unavailable. The hospital must have just seen him there with us and thought that was enough. But they didn't think about the emotional toll a heroin addicted mother would have on a young child. He was the breadwinner, and for the longest time, didn't know about my moms drug addiction. He always just thought she was depressed or something. Never understood mental health problems. Never thought to look in the bottom drawer of her nightstand. If he had, he would have seen her spoons with burnt bottoms and orange capped needles with dark splotches. If he had ever seen her in a short sleeve shirt, he would have seen her track marks. The ones she tried saying were from blood draws at the doctor. Yet the only doctor she saw was the guy on the street corner in the next town over.

My mom checked into rehab when I was 22. I was away for college when I got the phone call that she had gone missing from that rehab. My dad sounded worried. Being as at that time, it was relatively new knowledge to him that she was a walking bag of heroin. The next semester, I transferred to a school closer to home. I never moved back in with my dad, just made it work in this new house as best as I could. I had a good amount of money saved up from my time off between high school and college.

My mom still hasn't been found. Even three years later when I am almost finished with school and my dad is trying to find a new lover to fill her place.

They didn't have a very good marriage for the few years before she went to and disappeared from rehab. I'm not surprised they never filed for divorce though, because my father didn't care to talk about feelings. He was more of the auto-pilot type of person. Just grinded at work, came home to eat and shower, slept, and went right back to it.

It hurt me throughout childhood. All of it did. Seeing my mom sleep a majority of the day, my dad never wanting to engage in any bonding activities with me, dinner always consisting of microwave meals and my father constantly drinking a beer too many.

The first time I had to call 911 on my mom, she wasn't breathing and her lips were blue. I found her on the floor in the bedroom with a spoon on the ground next to her. I put it in the drawer and closed it before the first responders showed up. They let me ride with her in the ambulance and I got to see the nurses and doctors do everything they could once we arrived at the hospital. Being 16 at the time, I was terrified, but seeing how well the team of people worked, I could feel that I was meant to join them some day.

She is stunning. Seeing her walk into the kitchen tonight at Ashton's, my heart just about quit on me. Ever since I first laid eyes on her, I knew I wanted her in my life. In any sense of the word, I needed her. Her flashy, warm green eyes stood out against the crowd and almost had a tranquilizing effect on everyone who looked into them. I can't help but stare.

I know what just happened was crazy. But I need to talk to her. I need to clear the air from the last time we saw each other. Was it really only two weeks ago that I almost had everything I wanted? It felt like a *lifetime*.

Looking at her now, standing in the yard of Ashton's house, I can see her face lit up softly from the neighbor's lights, but I see her beauty. I see her hardships. I see her soul. Brooke was gorgeous. I catch her spinning her ring on her finger, she must be anxious. That's her tell. But I'd been asking myself why hadn't she texted me at all? Was she not interested?

I reach my hands up to my face, rubbing slightly to wipe away the worry. I finally take a breath and begin to speak. I want to fix this and hope I don't make it worse.

Chapter Six

Kasey's hand is both tender and strong at the same time, if that is even fucking possible. The way his attitude affects mine so easily is puzzling as he walks in silence with a sense of exigency, urging me to walk faster. Just from his touch my heart is dancing in my chest and I have butterflies in my stomach trying to escape.

He brings me to the furthest part of the yard, closest to the rackety, broken down fence marking the limit of the property. As we step up to the spot he's chosen to have this conversation, he slowly releases my hand, letting it return to my side leaving coldness behind.

Because I am standing, my anxiety can't escape through the steady bouncing of my leg so I am left to spin the rings around on my fingers. As I take a slow breath, filling my chest, he turns to look at me. Once again those penetrating blue eyes look deep into mine. He finally speaks after rubbing his face with his hands.

"First and most important, are you okay?" Pausing, he continues, "I know police officers can bring up some memories for you." He questions with the calmest, most endearing tone and matching look. He doesn't know details, just that I had trouble growing up.

I take my time responding. To be honest, that is a *very* loaded question. *Was* I okay? I hadn't even taken the time to process the police presence, only the accident itself and the feelings it brought up inside.

When we met a few years ago, we clicked instantly. A fire lit up in my body, and I can only hope the same happened to him. During the beginning of our 'friendship' we touched on our childhoods. But we never held the conversations long enough to get to the most violent, yet defining truths.

Standing just two feet away from him brought back all of the feelings I had been trying to suppress since the last awkward run in I had with him two weeks ago.

Finally I answer him, "Honestly, I haven't really had the time to ask myself that question so I'm not sure it would

be fair to answer you before answering myself."
Apprehensively looking into his eyes as I speak, hoping he can't hear the internal fluster I feel throughout my blood.

He turns away for a brief second, taking in what I just said. Sliding his hands in his pockets, rocking back and forth on his heels, and taking a deep breath, he faces away from me completely, my soul frozen without his gaze connected to mine. In one quick motion he turns to face me and takes a step in my direction, closing a majority of the gap that separated us when we first came outside.

He gently reaches a hand out to my face, silently asking for consent. I give a small smirk in return, giving him the approval he was looking for. His hand slowly caresses the side of my face, allowing his eyes to finally form a strong connection with mine.

"Brooke, where have you been?" He asks as his other hand wraps around my waist and pulls me closer, creating nothing more than an inch of space between our warm bodies. Soft concern lacing his eyes and voice.

I take a moment, allowing my heart rate that was spiked from the sudden act to settle slightly before answering him, "I thought you didn't want to hear from me. The last time we saw each other I was so... It was... I don't know." I stop, worried I'll say too much and scare him off.

He looks at me waiting for me to finish my thought. When I don't, he speaks to break the silence. "Why wouldn't I want to hear from you? You haven't left my mind since that night." I swear my legs instantly tremble, begging for assistance to continue standing.

I'm shocked, I truly thought he was happy we were interrupted that night two weeks ago. I thought it was just the alcohol in his blood that had started it in the first place. I look away to catch my breath and when I look back, he continues to voice his mind. "That night when you ran out, I thought I wouldn't see you again."

I quickly respond. "I wouldn't want that. I have been waiting to run into you but when I saw you tonight, I forgot everything I wanted to say to you and I thought you had my number blocked."

"I was giving you the time I thought you needed, I didn't want to seem... Overbearing." He speaks with such warmth I can't help but begin to melt into him, closing the gap between us even more.

Things with Kasey had always been anything but easy. Our conversations had a nice flow about them, but getting the time and privacy to actually have an extensive conversation was the hard part. Right now, standing so close to him, I felt at home. Home to me is something I've created, something greater, something more comfortable and meaningful. Since my home was broken, I searched in others to find it.

"I appreciate the intention, but I wanted nothing more than to talk to you. I'm sorry I didn't text you." I say to him, silently begging him to kiss me.

"Of course, and I'm sorry I didn't either. Maybe next time let's actually talk about things instead of holding assumptions?" He urges my agreement.

"I will try my best" I reply with a grin, the glow from the patio lights next door showing me his smile as I see it spread across his face. He releases me from his grasp and puts a hand around my waist, gently directing me to Ashton's back door and through the house. At the front door I turn back to him, "How are you getting home?" I ask, hoping he'll make a smart choice.

"I feel okay now, but I'll walk just to be sure." My eyes turn from worry to happiness, noting how he could sense my anxiety about him getting home safely. I nod, turning away from him and out the door as he stays behind to chat with Ashton before heading home himself.

I see my friends standing near the sidewalk, as I walk out and down the patio steps, Lily turns to me asking if I am ready to head out. With a voiceless cue, we turn and begin down the street.

Max and Janet's place isn't too far now and Janet whispers to Max something I can't hear. A few seconds later she speaks up, "Hey so we wanna continue this party at our place, who's down?" She says in a chipper tone, not happy with the speed at which the alcohol left her body.

"Fuck yeah" I practically shout, craving to use my coping skill to wash away the anxiety of talking with Kasey.

"Why not?" Lily chimes in.

"Sorry to disappoint, but I think I'm going to call it a night. I've got shit to do in the morning." Korey says with irritation. He agreed to help his mom clean out the garage bright and early tomorrow and is now regretting it.

"Ugh fine, lameass. But next time you better show." Max says but there's no heat to his words.

"I will, I will." Korey laughs back to him, giving him a half-assed fist bump.

"I'll hold you to that, punk," a laughing Max returns, giving him a slight shoulder shove. Passing Korey's he says his goodbyes paired with a hug for each of us, jogging up his walkway and disappearing into the safety of his home.

I turn to Lily, "So what happened with Ashton? Any good deets for us?" Hoping to lighten the mood while we continue our short trek.

"Well I went and talked with him, I swear he couldn't keep his eyes off me. But some girl kept trying to talk to him." She laughs, "It's actually funny, the few times she tried he would just turn a little away from her to focus more on me."

Janet and I laugh with her at the thought of sweet Ashton being a passive asshole. He's good at that when he needs to be but it's a pretty rare sight.

At Max and Janet's, us girls go to the couch and Janet cues up another summer playlist on Alexa, telling a story of some dumb shit she witnessed between some guys at the party. Max calls out for us, with freshly poured shots of Tequila sitting on the counter with our names on them.

He raises his glass and says, "For Charlotte!", licking the salt and pouring the Tequila into his mouth. We follow suit and all chew our limes together. Making faces and our giggles erupting when we are finally able to breathe.

It's already early in the morning but Max, energy still higher than ever, goes to pour us another round of shots only to let out a disappointed, dragged out groan. "Shiiit man, the bottle is empttyyy." The rest of us join him in the kitchen, seeing the crime that is the empty gallon.

"No way that was all us!" Janet exclaims, slurring her words. Max puts his arm around her shoulder and sways, "Nah baby, I forgot to grab a new one today." We all sigh and groan and laugh at what our largest trouble is right now.

"Well, that may be my cue to leave and let the love birds have their fun." I joke with them while making kissy faces.

"Hey, can I stay in the spare room? I don't want to walk home, I might find myself magically at Ashton's front door" Lily blushes at the thought of randomly timed, drunken sex.

"Yeah for sure, girl!" Janet responds before Max can counter.

"Awesome, you won't even know I'm here." She winks at the two, turning to me to give me a hug. "Will you be okay getting home or will *you* magically show up at Kasey's?" Her giant smile and wink makes my cheeks pink and I shy away.

"Yes, I'll be fine, I'm not impulsive about that like you are." I tease. I give her a hug and do the same with Max and Lily. Walking to the front door, I lace up my Converse and open the door, making sure to remind the drunk fucks to lock it when I leave.

The walk home from Max and Janet's is far and I don't mind the fresh air honestly. Besides, with the amount of alcohol in my body, walking seemed like the better option. I nearly fall down the last two steps of their apartment complex, steadying myself with a hand on the railing, I turn towards my aunt's house.

My phone buzzes in my back pocket and I reach to grab it, remembering I still need to change the tone, but thankful it is on vibrate right now. As I let the camera scan my face to unlock it, I see Korey's name with a message following it. As it finally opens and loads my texts, my eyes focus and I see that it was actually from *Kasey*, not Korey. Oh *shit*.

"Have you answered yourself yet?"

My head begins to spin from the alcohol, unsure how to respond. There are so many things I could say, but a lot of those are things I *shouldn't* say.

"currently trying to survive my walk home" I send after I laugh at my own stupidity. I'm almost to my aunts, several minutes after his original text, when my phone vibrates again, only this time not alerting me to a text but rather a phone call.

I immediately blush, wondering why he's calling me at 3:15 in the morning. The vibration is loud in the silent streets.

Just before the last ring, I slide the bar at the bottom to answer the call, stopping the vibration.

"Hey, Brooke." Kasey's raspy voice immediately calms my nerves and brings warmth across my stomach.

"Hey, Kasey. What's up?" I question, trying not to sound as drunk as I am.

"You said you were trying to *survive*, are you okay?" He pushes my comment.

"Oh yeah, I'm good, I was just making a joke." I slur my words as the Tequila makes my brain fuzzy.

"Just checking in, do you need a ride?" Damn his voice is hot when he's concerned and full of questions, which I suppose is fair because I am too, although mine are not about current times.

"No, I'm almost home." The slurring intensifies.

He takes a few seconds to think, I realize I have stopped walking since I answered the phone and begin to take steps again, one foot in front of the other, focusing on not tripping. He lets out a sigh, most likely feeling defeated I won't let him help. "Okay, get home safe. And Brooke? Let me know when you get there."

"I will." I hang up the phone, walk for another block, and turn my key in the lock, opening the front door. Stepping inside, I close and lock the door, untie my shoes and kick them off, and immediately open a text thread with Kasey.

"im home :)"

"Thank you" He replies instantly. I slide my phone in my back pocket and quietly step into the kitchen, grab a glass of water, and slink into my bedroom.

The house my aunt lives in now is not the same house as it was 10 years ago. Thankfully, shortly after Don was arrested, she started going to AA and working the steps. Three years after that she got a new, higher paying job and moved us to a nicer corner of town with nicer people and a nicer house and a nicer breeze. The best part of this house was the AC units scattered throughout it. Finally I get relief from the heat inside my own home when I visit.

I open the door to my room, plug my phone into the charger, and take off my shorts, leaving my shirt on. My bed is calling my name and I have never been so eager to climb in. I walk to the window in the corner of my room and open it along with my smell-proof box of weed. This was always the best cure for a night of drinking, even though it never actually helped. I smoke half a pre-rolled joint before walking to my bed. My head spins as I get under the covers, but the moment my head touches the pillow, I reach that level of drunk and content where you can sleep in any position.

Chapter Seven

Janet's text pulls me from thinking of the demons I'll face and I run through everything I remember. Yeah that was a lot. I feel like I need a few *months* of nothing, just to take it in. It wasn't necessarily a traumatizing event to me as I have been through so much already, but that didn't change the fact that it was a hard sight to see.

I scroll through my texts as I always do the morning after drinking to make sure I didn't send anything absurd and come across the texts with Kasey at the top with Janet's text below it. Why did I randomly tell him I was home? His reply didn't seem like he cared to know. Short with no emotion. Did I mean to text him? Did that text annoy him? I click on the text box to begin typing, writing and deleting several messages before finally deciding to just send it.

"hey, sorry about that... not sure why i told u i was home lol"

Finally, I remember to change the text tone and make it one that doesn't assault my ears. I lock my phone and set it on the bed next to me. My bladder is screaming at me to get the fuck up and let out all the liquid it was collecting, begging and threatening to explode if I didn't in the next few seconds. I roll the covers off of me and slide my legs over the bed, staying there while allowing my body to compensate for the sudden movements before I pass out on the way. I stand and my head pounds heavily. When I begin walking through the doorway of my bathroom I'm thankful I have my own attached to my room because *damn* that mirror is harsh this morning.

I take another refreshing shower and then put on some blue comfy pajama shorts, a gray t-shirt with wildflowers painted on, and a pair of fuzzy socks. With the AC on all the time my feet get chilly so why not be comfortable. I exit my room and turn for the kitchen, seeing my aunt relaxing on the couch with a mug of coffee in one hand and her phone in the other. I postpone food or caffeine to join her on the couch, sitting next to her and laying my head on the pillow in her lap. She sets her phone down and brings her free hand to my hair, brushing through the long blonde strands.

"How'd you sleep, love?" She takes a drink from her coffee waiting for me to answer. Our relationship has definitely improved in the last decade, thank God because I've needed her on my side.

"Like a rock, what are you up to today?" I smile as I answer her, even though she can't see my face.

"I'm thinking of taking an early day at work and spending some time on the beach, today is a special day." She says with dread, trying to sound sarcastic.

I had completely spaced it. She lost her sister 22 years ago. I lost my mom 22 years ago. It affects her more than it does me as I don't have any memories with my mother, I was too young to really understand what was happening when I was brought to live with Beverly. This day 22 years ago is why Beverly began struggling with alcohol, she needed a coping skill, as unhealthy as it may have been. I'm proud of her for finally working through all the suppressed feelings and I don't often share that with her.

"Aunty?" I sit up straight, off of her lap, and look at her. I take a breath and hold her free hand in mine. "I never really say this, but I am proud of you. I am proud of you for recognizing you needed help and for getting the help you deserved." She begins to tear up, shocked at the level of emotion I was offering so early in the morning. Well, early for me.

She squeezes my hand as she replies, "Thank you sweetheart, it feels good to hear that." She smiles affectionately. "I am proud of you, too. For standing up for yourself and waking me up from the terror that was going on in that house behind closed doors. You are strong."

"So are you." I give her a side hug and then stand up, walking to the kitchen and starting a pot of hot, steaming coffee. While waiting for my morning legal drugs, I pull out the rest of the breakfast ensemble.

I finish cooking my easy breakfast, pour myself a mug, and sit at the table scrolling through my phone while I try to eat as much as I can. Seeing everyone's posts on Instagram about the accident that took place outside Ashton's last night, I call out to my aunt. "Did you hear about Charlotte?"

"Yeah, I just saw something about it on Facebook. You weren't there were you?" She says as she stands up from the couch and walks to the kitchen sink, rinsing out her coffee mug and placing it in the dishwasher.

The great thing about staying with my aunt during summer break, is that we have an understanding. I am an adult and so is she, and we don't need to constantly keep each other updated on our whereabouts, as long as we check in and reach out if we think we, mainly me, feel we are in an unsafe situation.

"I was there but I didn't see it happen. I joined everyone outside right after though." I lock my phone and focus on my food.

"How are you feeling about it?" She carefully questions, not wanting to pry too much but still showing her love and care.

"Well, it was a tragedy, but honestly she made the decision. I feel for her and her friends but I'm also a little angry with her. That was a dumb choice." I pause before continuing, "Don't get me wrong, I will miss seeing her around when I visit, but it made me so mad thinking how that could have been you back then or one of my friends now." I twirl the remaining bites of egg on my plate, losing my appetite. I stand and rinse the plate out in the sink.

"I think those are all valid feelings, as horrible as it is, maybe this will remind people to be careful." She pulls me in for a hug as I sink into her. She kisses the top of my head and goes to her room to get ready for work. She has a pretty cool job nowadays. Doing some kind of office work, which is lame, but she works for a salary so she can come and go as she pleases as long as she hits her productivity quota every month.

I return to my room and take my place next to the open window, opening my weed box. I search for a pre-rolled joint, finding the one I must have started last night. I grab the lighter out of the box and bring the flame to the end *not* dangling from my lips, inhaling as they meet. The end of the joint takes the flame and begins to burn an orangey-red as I suck the flavor deep into my lungs. *This one's for you, mom.* I look out the window and enjoy the view of summer. Blue skies with no clouds, neighbors' houses hidden behind gentle tree cover, and a blue ocean in the near distance.

My phone vibrates and makes a small ping sound from my bed. I put the now finished joint back into the box and walk over to it. Picking up the phone it unlocks as it sees my face and shows a preview to the text that just came in.

"You don't remember our phone call?" Kasey had texted.

I panic inside, trying to wrack my brain around if we *did* talk on the phone and what I might have said in a moment of drunken weakness.

"honestly, not really.. did i say something stupid?" I text back, hoping for a good answer. While waiting for his response, I adjust the fan speed on my AC unit as I felt a whole 10 degrees hotter now than I did two minutes ago. Picking up my phone again, I text the group chat I have with my friends.

"proof of life please :) " I send, waiting for multiple texts to come in. I walk to the bathroom and brush my teeth. As I am scrubbing, I hear three notifications from my texts and two from Instagram. I finish brushing my teeth and rinse my mouth out with sink water, pulling all my hair into a hand-pony as I bend my head into the sink to spit. Two more text tones sound and I walk back to my bed, sitting upright against the pillows lining the headboard. I go through notifications in the same order they came in. Stopping myself from looking ahead.

"Alive and present" from Korey.

"what's shakin, bacon?" from Lily.

"Hello hello girllll" from Max.

Two Instagram reels from Janet, both are cat videos from her favorite account.

"breathing and well :) " Janet says in the group chat while I'm on Instagram, scrolling through the clips she sent.

Another text comes in and I see his name, I begin to feel uncomfortably warm again.

"Not at all, I was just checking to make sure you were good" from Kasey. I have always found it kind that even in our most off moments, he tries to show me he cares, without being too overwhelming. I smile at my phone, a dumb cheesy grin takes over my face. I shake my head and open the group chat to get my mind off Kasey.

"any plans today?" I send, hoping for a fun night. I lock my phone once again and stand up off my bed, grabbing my laptop from my desk and checking my emails making sure there's nothing from school for the upcoming quarter. Which is approaching much quicker than I'd like. I don't think it's fair you only get a few months off from school and then have to put your all in for the rest of the year. But I guess it is what it is.

"Yeah, we gonna go swimming, head count?" Korey replies a moment later. Everyone sends a confirmation text and with that, I stand. I dig through all the bathing suits I own, looking for my favorite one. A bikini with black, rather skimpy bottoms, and a teal, blue top that ties around the back. Covering that I chose to wear a black romper with thin straps and tiny pockets. I'm not sure the point in putting pockets in something if they won't even hold my phone. To finish the outfit I slip on my Converse and lace them up. Not doing too much makeup or anything special to my hair, I grab my beach bag, towel, and water bottle, and slide through the front door, walking to Max and Janet's.

When I get there, I don't knock. I walk inside and see Lily sitting on the couch with her short blonde hair in a half-up-half-down bun and a blue sundress that makes her eyes pop. She smiles as she sees me and waves me to join her while we wait for Korey to show up and Max and Janet to be ready.

"Hey love, how are you doing?" She asks, setting her phone down by her side.

"I'm doing good, how are you?" I reply, giving her a side hug.

"Not too bad, excited for a beach day. It's been too long since I was in the water." I laugh at her response because normally when we go to the beach she is laying on the sand trying to catch as much of a tan as she can before the rest of the group is ready to leave.

"As if you even swim!" I give her a shove.

She laughs as she responds. "Well today I *am* swimming!"

Max and Janet walk out of their bedroom dressed and ready at the same time that Korey walks through the front door. Korey takes over Max's normal job and pours some shots for everyone. This time choosing Vodka instead of Tequila because Max hasn't replenished the cabinet yet.

We all join around the island, grabbing the shot glasses and a cup of orange juice as our chaser. Excited to get the fun started, I raise my glasses and shout "For sunshine!" Everyone takes a small sip of juice, takes their shot in one big drink, and washes it down with the remaining OJ in their cups. We all put our shoes on, grab our bags and towels, and head for the beach.

Chapter Eight

    I grab my phone when I first wake up and reply to all the people that tried to get ahold of me. Saving the best for last, I open Brooke's text.

    "hey, sorry about that... not sure why i told u i was home lol"

    Was she really drunk enough that she didn't remember our phone call? I reply, asking exactly that. I worry now that she didn't make it home safely and I anxiously await her response to make sure she's okay. She immediately responds and my heart calms down.

I stand up out of bed and walk into my bathroom and start brushing my teeth. My hair looks a mess this morning, definitely wearing a beanie until I can shower out the alcohol of last night. I throw on my running shorts and a tank top, stepping out the front door to begin my run.

The trees sway in the breeze and help cool down the sweat seeping from my pores. My mind empties as the adrenaline sets in and I push hard through the last half mile. Finally, I click the button on my watch when I get a block away from home.

```
Workout Complete!
Summary:
4.2 miles
31 minutes
Average HR: 157 BPM
```

My room is comfortable to me. It embodies me as a man while still looking appealing to the average eye. My lighting isn't harsh, my bed has pillows, and my trash can isn't full and spilling into the rest of the room. That's more than I can say for my roommates. I slip into the shower after my run. There is only one thing on my mind the whole time.

Brooke.

I want to see her again but it needs to be more meaningful this time. It needs to be more than just running into each other at a party, it needs to have a purpose, be a special thing. Get your mind out of the gutter. I don't mean a purpose as in sex. I mean I need to know more about what goes on in her beautiful head. What has shaped her into who she is and how she handles herself.

My coping skill was just burying things for the longest time, it has improved but I am still guilty of bottling up when things get uncomfortable. That is probably a trait I got from my father. But I don't want to be that way. I don't want to be emotionally unavailable or a heroin addict. I don't want any of the traits from my parents. That's why I detached myself as soon as I could.

When I was old enough to, I started working long, hard hours to pull in money while waiting for college classes to start. Taking an extra year or so to save up. It was a difficult time but I managed pretty well. I tried really hard to distance myself from my family by keeping busy.

As distant as you can be for living in the same house that is. Luckily for me, when I was in college and things started going down the drain here, that being my mom going to rehab, my dad moved an hour or two away from our hometown. 'Trying to find bigger and better things' he'd said. Fine by me, that's more distance put between us without me needing to do anything.

Knowing vaguely that Brooke had a difficult upbringing and seeing her keep herself together shows me that it's possible to keep going despite the troubles. I've done a decent job so far but I still have my moments of self doubt. Everyone does, right?

I put on sweats and a T-shirt when I get out of the shower, my hair still damp but not dripping. My phone goes off and my heart beats against my chest, hoping it's Brooke.

"Party day?" From Charlie even though he's somewhere in the house I am also currently in. He is going to have to wait, I would rather see Brooke.

It would be nice to take Brooke out for dinner. A good time to get closer and know more about her. I can imagine sitting across from her, watching her emerald eyes lift with a smile, her hair draped around her face, and her warm laughter filling my ears. If she allows, ending the night with a kiss would be monumental. I want to take things slower than society deems normal. Create a meaningful connection before a physical one. She's worth more than just physical intimacy. She deserves the emotional side of it too.

I want to open doors for her, kiss her forehead good morning and good night, walk on the street side when I'm with her, protect her heart as best as I can. Protect her from others *and* herself.

I also, of course, want the physical connection. Brooke is fucking sexy. Her blonde hair and green eyes capture me instantly every time she looks at me. She is always wearing clothes that perfectly shape her already perfectly shaped body. The cutest thing about her is her Converse though. Always wearing them, like they're her emotional support shoes.

I sit down on the couch after cleaning up from breakfast, eggs and bacon, a classic. Eggs were scrambled with cheese and green onions of course. Arlo is sitting on the other side of the couch and nods my way when I sit down, "Hey, buddy," he says, drinking from his paper cup from the coffee shop down the street.

"Sup?" I ask, grabbing the remote and flipping through channels.

"I heard you saw Brooke the other day." He invites the conversation.

"Yeah at Ashton's. Why?" I reply, wanting him to press the topic so I can talk about her as much as possible.

"Oh no reason, I just know you secretly love her is all." He drinks from his coffee, "Not that it's actually a secret to anyone in this house." He laughs.

"I don't know what it is about her. She's just always been so...*There*. In my head, you know?" I say back, settling on a random documentary about pigeons on TV. It's just background noise, neither of us are going to be paying attention to it. I usually can't focus on the TV anyway.

"Maybe you just wanna bone her that bad." Arlo chuckles, and then, "What the fuck are we watching?" He questions.

"Fucking *birds* my guy." I laugh and take a breath, "Nah bro, it's more than that."

"I know man, just giving you shit." He stands, "Let me know when you're done with her so I can give it a shot." He sneers as he walks down the stairs and to his room.

"Asshole!" I shout after him, genuinely pissed off at him for thinking of Brooke as a disposable fuck doll.

"What are you doing tonight?" I send to Brooke after several minutes of debating what to say. Ideally, I'd ask her out in person, but I'm not sure when that will be and I want to see her as soon as possible.

I run upstairs to my room and sit at my desk and open my laptop, signing into my school website to double check I am enrolled in the right classes. This is my third time checking so I'm not sure why I'm doing it again. Third time's the charm I guess. Passing time, I pick up my room a little and straighten up a bit. Then plop myself onto my bed.

I must have fallen asleep for a short time because I woke up to a text from Brooke, my skin heating up just at the sight of her name.

Chapter Nine

We walk the short distance between the ocean and
Max and Janet's place, all stopping in our tracks the moment
our shoes touch the sand. Taking in a breath to appreciate the
aroma of the salt water and the heat of the sun. It's a toasty
93 degrees, somewhat muggy but not too bad. The
occasional cool, ocean breeze, with no clouds in sight.

Removing our shoes, and socks if we have them, we
allow our feet to sink into the hot sand.

"Where should we set up?" I ask no one in particular, hoping someone else will make the decision.

"How about down that way? Looks a little less busy." Max points to our right in the direction with not as many people and the jumping rock. It was midday on a Tuesday, sadly all the school-age kids, some middle school age, some high school age, and the rest college age, including us, decided to have a beach day while the real adults are stuck at work.

On our journey to the general area we chose, we pass a few groups of people we know, say our hellos and have small talk. As we get closer, I point out somewhere to lay our stuff down and the group nods in agreement.

I choose a spot that's about 20 feet from the water and 40 feet from the jumping rock, with somewhat even sand and a good view of the open horizon. Laying out our towels and setting down our bags, us girls take off the layer of clothes hiding our bathing suits. We pull out our sunscreen, lathering ourselves, not having time for skin cancer in this life. The guys pull their shirts over their heads and immediately sprint towards the water, begging for relief from the heat.

When the guys return, they towel dry and sit down in the sand. Max turns to Janet and asks her to put sunscreen on his back, she obliges happily and plants a kiss on his cheek before putting sunscreen on his back. Korey hands me a sunscreen bottle, silently asking me to do the same.

"And don't forget the kiss on the side." He smirks and winks at me.

"I'd rather puke." I joke back to him, opening the bottle and starting to put sunscreen on his back while he does his chest and face. Now that we are all covered in a healthy amount of sunscreen, we lay out on our towels and soak up the sun. Janet brought a flask with some vodka so we take turns sipping and then handing it off to the next in line. When it comes around to me for the fourth time, my phone buzzes on the towel next to me.

I pick up the phone, because of the sun my camera won't scan my face and I have to input my password. What an inconvenience. As it unlocks I see a text from Beverly.

"How are you doing sweetheart?"

I send a quick text back letting her know what I'm up to and that I am safe, not making any horrible decisions to add to her history of trauma on this day. Right before I lock my phone to return it to its rightful place at my side, it pings again. Before opening the text I take another big gulp of the room temperature liquor, passing it on to Lily next to me.

"What are you doing tonight?" The text comes in from Kasey. Instantaneously my cheeks get red, out of panic I lock my phone and set it down. Wondering why I fall apart every time he comes up in my day.

Max looks at me as the smile on my face begins to die down. "Who's got you blushing over there girl?" He presses the matter.

"Oh that's *got* to be Kasey, there's just no other option." Janet says, sliding her glasses to the top of her head and sitting up on her arms to get a better look at the cherry color painting the sides of my face.

"No it's just my aunt." I say, looking towards the jumping rock. Wanting to avoid talking about Kasey I continue, "She is asking what I'm up to, today is *that* day."

Lily doesn't fall for that one. She's both kind and curious. "Brooke, I know about today, but that doesn't ever get an emotional response out of you, especially getting hot and heavy."

"Now that'd be weird as fuck." Korey gags at the twisted thought.

"Oh shut up." I give Korey a glance and smack his arm playfully. "Fine, it was Kasey. But I don't know what to say." I reply honestly.

"Girl! Go out with him!" Lily gets excited.

"If you don't then you don't get any of our Tequila for a week!" Janet shouts sarcastically, joking with a hint of truth to her threat.

Korey snatches my phone up off my towel and tries to enter my password, I'm able to swipe it away and stick my tongue out at him before he can get it unlocked. "Oh you definitely have to go out with him if I can't see the message. Is it spicyyy?" He teases, smiling at me.

My whole friend group has always been very supportive of me 'finding love' as I haven't really had a solid relationship since we graduated high school. Don't get me wrong, I've had my fair share of fun, but nothing ever worth my time and effort for something real. Except Kasey. I always look back and wish we could have jumped into each other's presence faster from the start, but something always got in the way.

"No! It's not *spicy*! Nothing like that has happened since that party a few weeks ago. Even then nothing really happened." I roll my eyes at the memory of being interrupted that night.

"So what are you two doing tonight? Can we spy from a distance?" Janet lowers her sunglasses back to her eyes, her crystal blue eyes hurting from the harsh sun, and takes a drink from the flask.

"I haven't even responded. I don't think I want to hang out with him tonight. And even if we were, no you cannot *spy*, he knows your faces." I blush again at the thought of spending time alone with Kasey.

"Why are you so reluctant?" Korey questions, staring at me for an answer.

I stand up and throw my sunglasses onto my towel dramatically. I take a few steps away from them, turn back to see their eager eyes, and then run to the water. Diving as soon as the water reaches my mid-thigh, feeling my warm body split the cool water. The ocean on a hot day is the most refreshing thing I can think of. Even more than a hangover-curing shower.

When I resurface, pushing the hair away from my face, I see Janet, Max, Lily, and Korey running to join me in the salty, gentle waves. They mimic my actions and glide through the water towards me. Treading water with my closest friends reminds me of how we may grow up and away, but we always come back to our roots.

We tread the water together in silence for a few minutes before Lily turns to face the shore.

"Well, I swam." She dips her head under the water one more time before slowly swimming at the surface back to the sand. Korey and Max join her after Max gives Janet a quick peck on the lips.

I turn back to the rest of the open ocean as Janet begins to speak. "Real talk. What are you thinking?"

I look at her, "I don't know." I squint in her direction, "I want to see him but I always get so nervous around him. It's like I forget how to be my normal self."

"Well, baby steps. Do something in public with him tonight and work from that. I'm sure we will end up at Blazer's tonight at some point so if something happens just come to us."

"Or at your place, if Max buys more liquid gold that is." I laugh as we both turn and swim to shore.

As I walk out of the water with Janet, our feet dig into the hot sand with each step, making the walk back to the towels and our friends breathtaking, and not in the 'ahh beautiful' way.

I sit on the towel and take a long drink of my cold water, setting it to the side of my towel, buried in the sand just a little to protect it from the sun. I pull my phone up to my face and squint, typing in my password and opening my text messages. I suppose I should answer Kasey before he regrets asking.

"no plans yet, you?" I type and press send, hoping to sound nonchalant and not overly excited. Moments later he responds. Before reading it I'm handed the flask with a little bit of Vodka left. I finish it off and check the message.

"I was hoping we could get together" Reading the words practically made me pass out. I hand the phone to Janet, holding the back of my hand to my forehead in an exaggerated fashion.

"*Eek!* Brooke, *please* say yes!" she squeals. Korey takes my phone and reads the text, also encouraging me to indulge in some fun.

I take the phone back and draw a breath before responding. **"sure, when do u wanna meet?"** I send it before I doubt myself. Drinking more of my water to cool off, Lily starts plotting.

"How's five?" He texts back within a minute.

"You should go to Blazer's. That way we can watch! Or what about that restaurant on Meridian? Oh! Oh! What if you went to his place?" She gives a devious smirk and winks at me.

I roll my eyes, "We'll see what he says. You guys ready to get out of the sun for a bit?" I stand, shaking off my towel. They all nod and stand, shaking their towels, drying their hair, and grabbing their bags. We start the walk back to Max and Janet's apartment.

As we pass the market just down the street from our destination, Max slips inside and buys a gallon of Tequila and a small bag of limes. "In preparation of celebration" he says when he walks out and gets a glance or two from the crowd.

"Celebrating what?" I ask him.

"You getting laid by your lover boy, *duh*!" He says with enthusiasm.

I shake his arm off my shoulder and roll my eyes, "Oh fuck off, Max. We are just hanging out."

"Just *hanging* out. Sure." He winks at me.

Janet lets out a loud laugh and we finish the walk. I can't wait to get inside the cold apartment and start drinking the poison to calm my nerves.

When we walk in the door, we are hit by the cold rush of air that the AC is working overtime to produce. Max pours everyone a shot and we gather around. Taking our shots, we all have the same reaction, shivers from lukewarm yet burning Tequila sliding down our throats, thankful for the lime.

"Alright, y'all. I'm gonna head home and get ready." I say grabbing my things and heading for the door.

"Good luck, Brookey!" They say in unison.

Chapter Ten

    The walk home felt faster than usual, it was either the liquor, the giddy butterflies I felt in my stomach, or the fact that I was actually walking a little faster to rush back into the safety of the AC in my home.

    When I unlock the door, I see my aunt standing in the kitchen cooking something on the stove. I walk inside, take off my shoes, and set my bag down on the couch.

"Hey, I'm home!" I shout so she can hear me over the vent fan on the underside of the microwave.

"Hey, sweetie! How was the beach?" She yells back, flipping the grilled cheese in the pan.

"It was fun, how was your day? What beach did you end up going to?" I ask, realizing I hadn't seen her earlier.

"Oh I skipped the beach and decided to treat myself to the movies and then a little shopping. Your mother loved the movies more than the ocean, which I always thought was *insane*." She laughs at the sweet memory of my mother.

I laugh with her despite the slight mourning of someone I never really knew. "Did you buy anything worth sharing?" I ask, intrigued to see her new purchases.

"Yeah I bought a cute sundress! Want to see it?" She flips the finished grilled cheese onto a plate with the spatula, turns off the stove, and sets the plate at the table.

"Is that even a question?" I smile at her.

She opens the orange, glossy paper bag on the dining room table and pulls out and holds up a beautiful light green dress that would end just above her knees with a lightly colored pattern of pink flowers. The dress had one inch thick straps that wrapped over the shoulders with a zipper on the back.

"Beverly!" I gasp, "That is *gorgeous!*" I run my hand along the fabric and feel the silky smooth cloth as it falls free. "This would look amazing with those nude flats you have!"

She blushes, "Thank you, honey. I'm excited to find an occasion to wear it."

71

"Go find yourself a hot date! It's been years since you were in the game!" I insist. She hasn't seen anyone in a long time. For three years after Don was arrested she was practically celibate. Then found someone she was interested in. They were very cute together but ended up fizzling out after a few months. She hasn't so much as looked at a man since then.

She folds the dress and puts it back in the bag. Sitting down at the table, she takes a breath before speaking. "Yeah I know, but it's scary out there." She laughs, "Don't rush me, girl. On my own time," and smiles at me.

"I know, I know. No pressure here." I give her a hug and start walking to my room, grabbing my bag off the couch on the way.

I grab my phone out of my bag and set it on my bed, along with the rest of my essentials. Wallet, keys, chapstick, and sunglasses. I unlock my phone while applying my chapstick and open my texts with Kasey to see what the plan is. *Shit*. I never responded to him.

"hey sorry i didnt realize i never responded.." I dread his response, my mind overthinking that he will cancel because I was horrible and never confirmed our plans. He probably has other plans by now. I'm not sure why he'd want to see me in the first place.

My phone vibrates, "Don't stress it's all good :) You still want to hangout?" I'm shocked to see he's still interested.

"yeah i'd love too, where do u wanna meet?" I panic after I press send. Why do I worry so much about what he thinks about me? Or care if I sound too eager? He's the one asking me out.

"How's drinks at Blazer's and then dinner at Avanti's?"

My palms get sweaty with excitement at the thought of a sit-down dinner with Kasey.

"yeah sounds good :) see you at 5?"

I lock my phone and walk into my bathroom, desperately needing to wash the salt water, sunscreen, and sunshine off my body.

I turn on the shower and pull a clean towel from the cabinet next to my door, undoing the ponytail my hair was in. When the water is warm enough, I take off my clothes and step under the steady stream of water.

After my energizing shower, I step out and pull my hair into the towel to keep it from dripping all over the floor, I start my makeup process.

Finishing my makeup, I take the towel out of my hair and blow dry it, using the curler to put more beach wave curls in the blonde strands. I walk over to my closet and start the painstaking process of choosing an outfit. Needing some assistance, I open my phone and call Janet.

"Hey, boo. What's up?" Janet sounds cheerful through the phone and I can hear some music in the background.

"I need help" I fake a cry, "What the hell do I wear to go see Kasey?"

She gives a squeal, "Oh *girl!* Wear that light pink dress, the one with the loose sleeves!"

"That seems too fancy." I say while pulling out the dress anyway, admiring the flowy material with loose sleeves that travel to about my elbows.

"Okay.. What about that dark green one? That shows a little skin on the sides? Where are you guys going anyway?"

"Oh yes. That's the one!" I retrieved the army green dress from my closet, with its flashy sides and V cut neckline. "We are going for drinks and then Avanti's for dinner." I'm debating skipping on the drinks though, it sounds like the group is at Blazer's and I don't want to run into them while trying my hardest to impress Kasey.

"Oh hell yes! That dress will fit the vibes so well!" She wishes me luck and hangs up the phone. When I see the call had ended, I realize I had missed a text from Kasey when I was in the shower.

"It's a date :) "

I lace up my shoes and lock the door on my way out. Sitting in the driver seat of my old car, I open my phone and start typing to Kasey. When I saw that "it's a date" text I about shit my pants. The thought of going on a date with *Kasey* was absurd to me. Was he really interested in me? Enough to go for a date and not just a one night stand?

"mind if we skip Blazer's?" It's a quarter to five so there should be enough time to coordinate skipping drinks, it's not like there is a reservation at the bar.

"That's okay with me. Meet at the boardwalk then? It's close enough to Avanti's" he replies quickly.

"**it's a date :)** " I send, hoping he'll see the humor in mocking his text earlier and not think it was a stupid attempt. As I drive to the boardwalk, I can't help but run through a million far-fetched scenarios.

What if this is all a joke? What if he's not going to show up and he's baiting me? What if I overdressed? What if he brought friends to embarrass me? What if it goes amazingly well?

I pull into the parking lot and spot his car a few spaces down. I take a drink from my water bottler and a few deep breaths before getting out of my car. I figure he will see me if I go and stand a few yards away from his car and look out into the busy boardwalk.

Sure enough, just a few moments after I chose where to stand, he comes up behind me, placing a hand on my waist. I spin around, my first intrusive thought is that this isn't Kasey and just some creep trying to cop a feel. When I lock eyes with him, a smile spreads across my face, flashing my white teeth and making my cheeks pink.

"Hey, Brooke. You look.." he pauses, his eyes scanning me up and down, "incredible." His eyes do another search of me and he takes a deep breath.

"Hi, you look.. Just as good." I say, having a hard time not just staring at him. He's wearing black Vans, a pair of light washed jeans that make his eyes breathtakingly blue, and a black t-shirt that lets his tattoos see the sunshine. He's wearing a thin silver chain around his neck, under his shirt but still showing at the collar, and a matching silver bracelet. Just *wow*. He looked *hot*. How was I going to make it through this date with him just existing like this.

He chuckles, "You want to walk around for a bit? Dinner isn't until seven o'clock." Kasey looks out to the buzzing boardwalk, sun shining low in the sky.

"You made reservations..?" I ask, timid and shocked.

"Of course I did, I wanted to make sure tonight was worth your time." He gives an encouraging smile.

Walking around with Kasey is strange. Knowing that he is here for me, no matter his intentions, is a great feeling. Knowing he chose me to be here with him gives me such a boost of confidence.

But at the same time there is part of me nagging to know his intentions, or at least what he claims them to be. We choose a bench facing the water and sit next to each other, a comfortable distance between us.

"Why'd you ask me out tonight?" I don't make eye contact, staring into the water and fidgeting with the rings on my fingers while my hands rest anxiously on my lap.

"I've been wanting to ask you out for a while now, waiting for the best time but it never really happened. So I took a chance." He leans forward on the bench, turning slightly towards me, silently begging me to look at him. "I'm really happy you said yes," he smiles.

"So am I," I look at him, "But it caught me off guard. I just couldn't shake the thought that you were trying to play a trick on me or something."

His eyes got softer than I thought they could, "I would never play games with you. Except for bar games, I

76

could kick your ass in those." He throws his head back in laughter as I chuckle and smile.

He stands and reaches a hand out to me, I take another look at him, all of him, and grab his hand standing with him. "We have a bit of a walk to Avanti's. Wanna get going?" He doesn't let go of my hand all the way to the restaurant. Standing at the hostess stand, he moves his hand to the small of my back and gives the young lady at the post his name. We follow her to our table.

I'm amazed as we approach our table, realizing it is in the back corner of the building with a view of the front door. I'm even more amazed when he pulls my chair out for me to sit and then takes a seat for himself with his back to the door.

"I may have noticed you always find yourself in the corner facing the door," without me asking he answers my curiosity, "I figured I should keep it that way to make you comfortable."

I'm awestruck. He had noticed this tiny-to-others yet huge-to-me fact. He's right, I feel a lot more comfortable. I can feel the fear and anxiety seeping out of my feet and into the floor. "That might be the nicest thing someone has done for me without being asked." I thank him as the waitress brings our waters, takes our drink orders, and brings rolls of bread as an appetizer.

Chapter Eleven

I excuse myself to the restroom while Kasey is paying the bill, stepping away from the table I can feel his eyes staring into me. I use the toilet, obviously, and then check myself in the mirror as I wash my hands. My cheeks are red from laughing so much during dinner, they are sore, too. I turn the water to cold and soak my hands, dry them off, and then pat my cheeks to cool them down. After finishing up my self-check, I walk back into the dining room of the restaurant, finding Kasey on his phone. As I walk up, he locks it and sets it down, giving me his full attention, making me feel like the only woman in the restaurant.

"You ready to go?" He asks me.

I nod, "Yeah, let's get out of here." I smile at him. He stands and replaces his hand in the small of my back, lightly guiding me to the outside air.

It is late evening now so the air is a little cooler than when we arrived for dinner, the sun still giving off some light, and the water reflecting what's left of it.

"Do you have anywhere to be soon?" I stop walking when we reach the edge of the boardwalk, overlooking the water, hoping he can stay with me for a while longer. Unsure of when I'll get a night like this again.

"Nope, I'm all yours." He smiles and puts his arm around my shoulder, leaning against the edge of the boardwalk next to me. I blush at his comment.

"What's next on the agenda?" I pray for anything that includes him.

"Hmm…" He looks at the action surrounding us. "Night swimming." He says matter-of-factly.

I look around, "Here? There's so many people, and I don't have my bathing suit." I laugh at the spontaneous plan he has. Being spontaneous is probably one of the things I love most, although it may not always be the best thing I should be doing.

"Stop at your place for a bathing suit, I'll run home and grab mine, and then I'll pick you up? You don't live too far from me." He suggests and I happily take him up on the offer. I turn towards our cars and he follows me, turning it into a race of who gets to their car first. "I'm gonna win, ya know." He shouts, picking up the pace.

"Never in a million years!" I shout back, turning my quick steps into faster ones.

I park my car in the side of the driveway I have deemed mine and run inside as fast as my legs will allow. I want some extra time to prepare so I need to move quickly. I burst inside the door after my house key cooperates, allowing my entry. My aunt sitting on the couch jumps with shock.

"Sorry! I'm in a bit of a rush!" I say as I speed past her and into my room. Rummaging through my drawers I find my all black bikini and soft gray shorts. Changing into them I hear my aunt yell back to me, "Everything okay?" Concern in her voice.

"Yes I'm good! Great actually! Just need a wardrobe change!" I yell back to her, grabbing my light yellow, thin, long sleeve crop top out of my closet and throwing it over my head, pulling my hair from it to rest on my back.

"Where are you off to?" She asks, her voice quieter than a yell now because she's watching me from the doorway.

"I'm out with a friend and we wanted to go swimming so I had to change. He's on his way to pick me up." I say breathless with excitement.

"*He's* on his way?" She raises an eyebrow at me while I take off my socks and replace them with slippers.

"Yes, *he*." I smirk, not wanting to give her all the details. To be fair, there was still time for this to go poorly and I don't want to get her hopes up. She's been bugging me about when I am going to get a 'boyfriend', as all family members normally do.

"Well, be safe. I know I don't need to lecture you but I still need to say it." She walks to me and gives me a warm hug, "I love you, sweetie." She turns to leave.

I laugh and call to her "I love you, too. You're next for going on a date!"

Slipping into my bathroom I give myself another glance in the mirror as my phone buzzes in my pocket.

"I'm here if you're ready :) "

I 'heart' the message, slide my phone back into my pocket, grab my towel and keys, and head to the front door.

"Have fun!" My aunt calls from the kitchen as I walk through the door.

"I will!"

Kasey and I spend a majority of the short drive talking about where we will be going when summer break is over. It makes me a little sad to think we might not be going to the same place. We've never really had a chance to speak about our college experiences and what we were going to school for.

"Well I am getting ready to graduate here soon. I took some time off before going back to school" he says, taking the last turn before the parking lot for the beach. "I went with nursing, I've always liked helping people and this felt like a good way to go about it. Especially since I don't get queasy around blood."

"That's a good field for you, you've got kind eyes that could heal wounds." I am shocked that I spoke before I thought.

He looks at me briefly as he pulls into the parking lot, "Thank you, Brooke." We pull into a spot and the car slows to a stop, putting the car in park he turns to me, "So what did you end up majoring in? What's your plan?"

I am always hesitant to bring up my major because people that chose this major usually always have trauma involving the law. "It took a bit to decide. I debated being a nurse, a doctor, a lawyer. But I finally landed on majoring in criminal psych. Not sure which path exactly I want to take but the degree comes with options." I reply, hoping he won't question why in detail.

We stand up out of the car and grab our towels. Walking towards the water he continues the conversation, "Have you graduated?" Taking the steps onto the sand we remove our shoes.

"I'm on track to graduate a little early, actually. I also took some time before going back to school and have a few more classes. I should be good to graduate in December."

"That's amazing! I'm proud of you for going strong and getting out of there early!" He exclaims as we get closer to the shore. We come to a spot and he speaks again, "Wanna set our stuff here?"

"Yeah this is good. Let's get in that water. I'm *dying* to taste the salt!" I yell excitedly as I peel my shirt over my head and slip out of my shorts. I catch Kasey staring at my breasts as the shirt comes off. I turn to set my clothes down and when I look back at him, his shirt is on the ground and I am impelled to look him up and down.

With his shirt removed I can now see the muscular body his clothes normally hide. His person is sleek yet full. Outlined abs that don't seem rock hard or uncomfortable to lay on. His tattoos against his tan skin, a butterfly here, a design there, words here and much more filling the space on his chest and stomach. I am now more able to see where his neck tattoo starts in the space between his collarbone and shoulder, trailing up to end behind his right ear.

My body shudders with excitement and I try to bury it, "Let's do this!" Running towards the water without giving him a moment to speak. I hear him following me as I plunge into the water, diving in and allowing the water to once again trace my body.

I come up for air at the same time that he does, looking at him and seeing his smile reflect the moonlight that is allowing us to see. "You're absolutely gorgeous. Do you know that?" He speaks, breaking the silence. "I haven't stopped thinking about you."

I swim towards him, slowly closing the gap of salt water between us. Without breaking eye contact, I move my arm from under the water. Bringing my hand up and resting it on his cheek softly. "It's hard to see sometimes, but I feel it occasionally." I say, letting him into my headspace.

I see his cheeks flush as soon as my hand touches his face, he shyly turns his head away and I guide it back towards mine with my hand. My heart is racing, this is more forward than I usually allow myself to be with someone I am interested in. He gives me confidence. And seeing he has a similar reaction to our touch as I do only boosts that confidence.

One of his arms wraps around me and closes the gap between us completely. His other arm mirrors mine on his cheek as he does it. My breasts bump into his chest and a small gasp of air leaves my mouth, surprised by the sudden movement.

My hand on his cheek moves to join my other wrapped around his neck. My eyes are caught by the trap of his ocean blue eyes, his lips crash into mine with both a force and tenderness I have never felt before. He lets out the air from his lungs and draws in another breath, only intensifying the kiss. His tongue teases my lips, begging for entry. I allow it as our mouths connect us, sending surges of electricity through my whole body.

His hand leaves my cheek and finds its way to the back of my head, tugging just a little on my hair. A small moan leaves my mouth as he kisses me harder. My mind is spinning yet blank at the same time. My legs wrap around his waist and I can feel him hardening under his green swim trunks. His lips leave mine and lonely coldness takes their place. They move to my cheek and slowly trail down. I lean my head back giving him access to my neck. The second his mouth finds it I can feel myself beginning to lose control.

He only stays there for a few seconds before bringing my face back to his, kissing my lips passionately one more time. I pull away, out of breath and tingling, looking into his eyes. "Kasey.." I start.

"Yes, Brooke?" He answers with desperation and rasp in his voice. Innocent and lustful eyes.

"I've missed you." I pant.

"I've missed *you*." He replies, just as breathless.

Chapter Twelve

Back on the beach, Kasey and I grab the towels we
brought. Watching him towel dry his brown curls makes me
giddy. The muscles in his back contract with each movement
of his arms in an attempt to rid his hair of the salt water. I
can't help but stare, letting my eyes trace every inch of him.
He slowly slides his shirt back on when he's finished. I do
the same, leaving my shorts off because wet pants are never
fun.

"Ready to head home? It's getting a little late." He asks as he gathers his keys and towel from the sand, checking the time on his phone and looking at me. His eyes gain lust once again when he sees me without my shorts on.

"Sadly, yes." I give him a smile. We turn towards the car and he grabs my hand in his. It feels as if my hand has always *belonged* in his.

We throw our towels into the backseat of his white Jeep, sitting in the front and buckling our seatbelts. Before he begins to drive, he looks over at me. "So, have you answered yourself?"

It takes me a moment to process his question. Finally remembering our talk from the backyard at Ashton's party, I reply.

"Yeah actually, I finally have. I'm doing good. It was heavy but I've put in a lot of work to get through the stuff that happened to me. So it wasn't as triggering as I thought it'd be. Thank you for checking on me." I smile at him, placing my hand on his leg.

He smiles back at me, "I can't imagine not checking on you." He puts the car in reverse and backs out of our spot, heading towards my house to drop me off.

The whole drive there he had his hand on my leg, occasionally squeezing it with a hint of desire. Pulling up to my house, we sit in the car for a few minutes. Just taking in how much fun our night was. How fun our *date* was. I look over to him, "Thank you for tonight. I had an amazing time." We smile big at each other. Our eyes locked on one another, dreading to break away.

"Can I take you out again?" He asks with eagerness.

I roll my eyes, "Of course you can." With that he kisses my cheek goodnight and I get out of his car, turning back to him when I am just a few steps from my front door. He waits until I am inside to drive off.

The second I close the door I lean against the back of it, cliche but it's a must. My legs feel like they're going to give out and I'm going to fall over flat on my face if I don't. The way I felt when hanging out with Kasey was... Comfortable, to say the least. I also just realized this is the first time I have felt this good about a social activity without drinking. I guess you could say there was some growth happening. I check the time on my phone as I head towards my bedroom. It's a little after midnight and my aunt is fast asleep. I want to share with her some of the details of my night but it will have to wait until tomorrow. Instead, I walk over to my bathroom and do my night routine. Grabbing my phone on the way to my window, I text Janet.

"GIRL you'll never guess" I send, wanting to spill the beans.

While I wait for her response, I spark up a joint and open my window. My phone vibrates after a few moments. **"how was it???? I need TEAAA"**

"it was INCREDIBLE i feel like im gonna pass out" I reply, taking another drag of my weed.

"did you guys fuck???" Straight to the point with this one, that's part of the reason I love her.

"no we didnt but god DAMN i wanted it. seems like he's in no rush, wants to take me out again so i assume he wants to do it

the 'right' way :) " I walk in circles around my room, wrapping my head around what tonight made me feel inside.

Right off the bat I feel exhilarated. Recharged. Excited. Loved. But at the same time I feel scared. Ashamed. Exhausted. It's hard to process feelings without the help of someone else. But I'll try my best with this.

I want to go all in and let myself fall as hard and fast as I can. With my history it is hard to give all in sexually to someone I care about. One night stands and meaningless flings are easy for me, I just bury the intrusive thoughts. But with Kasey, I don't want to bury anything, I want to feel it *all*. I want to let him in and help me. That's easier said than done. My thoughts are interrupted by two texts on my phone. I put the joint out, change into my pajamas, climb into bed, and check my phone.

"that's so exciting girl i'm happy for you!!" From Janet, I love having her support, it's always been such a special thing to me. I 'heart' her message and open the rest of my texts.

"Can't wait for next time" From Kasey, with a kiss face emoji. Gah, my heart.

I immediately reply, "i hope it's soon" I send a kiss face emoji right back. Holding my phone to my chest for a few seconds I can't help but let out a big breath accompanied by a smile and a laugh. Heat taking over my face.

I plug my phone in and make a last minute decision to take a shower. High showers are healing. Even more so than hangover showers.

I slide off my shirt and bathing suit, kicking them in the direction of my laundry basket in the corner and turn on the water to let it warm up.

After my shower, I towel dry my hair and put it into a braid so it will be easier to manage in the morning. Finally I am ready for bed, climbing under the covers, I fall asleep rather quickly while the memories of tonight run through my head.

I am aware of the light seeping through my blinds before my eyes open. For once, there is no throbbing headache to go with it. Just a dry mouth from the joint before bed. I reach over to my nightstand and grab my water bottle, taking a long drink of ice cold refreshing water. Thankful I filled it last night. I sit up in bed grabbing my phone as I set the water bottle down.

I woke up to a few texts from the group.

"Plans today?" Max had sent an hour earlier.

Janet had replied, even though they live together, **"beach and bar?"**

Korey also responded, **"YES PLS"**.

Lily must be sleeping still, it was only 10:30 in the morning.

I start typing my response, **"when and where my loves"** and hit send. I lock my phone and use the toilet, washing my face and doing my morning routine. When I'm finished I slip out of my room and head towards the kitchen. Still feeling hot from my endeavors last night.

Walking up to the coffee pot and grabbing a mug from the cabinet above, I pour myself a strong one. My aunt is sitting on the couch with her coffee, same as always. I walk to her with my cup and sit next to her on the couch. We sit in silence for a little while, drinking and scrolling through our phones. Neither of us are totally awake yet.

The silence ends, "So how was your date?" She locks her phone and turns her attention to me, ready for my narration of last night.

"It was actually so fun! You were asleep when I got home and I was sad I couldn't share it with you then." I take a sip of my coffee before continuing. "We swam until we were wrinkly and then he drove me home. We may have kissed…" I raise an eyebrow and smile, showing my happiness with the events that took place last night.

"*May* have? Hmm," she smiles back, "What did you two do before swimming?" She finishes her coffee awaiting the rest of the story.

"He made *reservations*. For Avanti's! I was shocked when I found out." Too excited to sit still I stand and fill her mug with more coffee, not adding any creamer because that's how she likes it.

"Oh! How fancy!" She gleams with enthusiasm. "I'm glad it went well and you made it home safely." She kisses the top of my head and walks towards her room to get ready for the day.

Chapter Thirteen

I roll over in bed and face the window, the blinds are open and the sun is bright. Did last night really happen? When I dropped Brooke off at her house, I drove home with the biggest most gleeful smile I've worn in a very long time. The smile continued until I climbed into bed. Waking up this morning, I'm craving more. I want to get to know her in every way. Man, even if she hated me at the end of our run at least I would have had the time with her.

Things got heated in the water for a few minutes and as much as I wanted to carry her out and bring her home with me to finish what we started, I wanted to move slowly with her more. It's important to me that she doesn't feel pressured.

My phone vibrates and I see a text from my father.

"3 years today. You holding up okay?" It reads.

It's been three years on the dot since my mom 'disappeared' from rehab. I'm still convinced she ran away with some guy from rehab and has either already overdosed and put herself in a coma under some Jane Doe name, or she is close to it.

"Yeah I'm good. You?" I send and lock my phone. I really don't care about today too much. My mom made her own choices and while it's sad and difficult to have an addict as a mother, I spent way too long feeling sorry for myself. Don't get me wrong, I still feel sadness and guilt over it, I just don't let it control my life.

I finally jump out of bed and walk to my dresser, grabbing some clothes to wear on my run, putting on my watch, and walking out of my room. Charlie is sitting at the table eating lunch when he says, "You're up late."

"Yeah I know, slow morning. Run time, though!" I say over my shoulder as I run out the door. Desperate to get a sweat in.

I jog down the street, past the coffee shop, past the mechanic shop named Karing Kars that Korey's family owns, past the main gas station in town, and do a loop through the neighborhood adjacent to mine. I debate going down to the beach but I don't think running in the sand is particularly fun. The whole loop is about four miles and my times are getting better. I'm not training for anything but I think it's fun to watch as my body gets conditioned and goes through changes.

The weather today is nice, not harsh or dramatic. Blue skies and sunny, and it will definitely get even warmer as the day goes on. The sidewalk I'm running on could use some TLC, the trees lining the sidewalk and street are showing off their roots in the rudest way, cracking the concrete and screaming for fresh air. I get to the crosswalk a block from my house, signaling the end of my run.

```
Workout Complete!
Summary:
4.2 miles
35 minutes
Average HR: 156 BPM
```

Walking in the front door, I'm greeted by Arlo getting ready to leave.

"You gonna snag Brooke or do I have to?" He asks, taunting me with his 'fuck boy' ego.

"Don't fuck with her, dude." I say, my blood warming.

"Or what?" He snickers. "You gonna fight me for her? She's just another bitch I can fuck." He laughs with the last part, making my blood officially boil. His attitude becomes more aggressive every day.

I take a breath, delaying my urge to knock him out with my fist. "Just don't, man." I reply. The last thing I want is this twat fucking things up with Brooke and I. We are just getting started.

I need time to do things right and win her the right way. If there even is a right way.

Arlo gets lots of girls. But they never last. He says it's because he doesn't want commitment but I'm pretty sure it's just because he's an asshole and can't keep it in his pants. His last girlfriend lasted no more than two months because he saw someone 'hotter' at a party. He acts like a freshman in college even though he'll be a senior this year. How he made it this far in school is beyond me.

"Whatever." He finishes the conversation and walks out the front door, slamming it behind him.

"Ignore his ass." Charlie says from the couch.

"He pisses me off, dude." I say, sitting on the other end of the couch.

"He'll either flunk out this year and move back home or graduate and move somewhere else, just get through the next two semesters." He drinks his beer, "Unless you move first after you graduate. Any ideas on where you wanna work?"

"Nah I haven't decided yet. Haven't put a ton of thought into it either because school is just a lot lately." I reply.

He nods his head in agreeable, gets up from the couch, and says, "Truly bro, ignore him."

"I'll do my best." I say back as I stand and walk to the fridge, grabbing a much needed beer and cracking it open.

I get in the shower at the same time my phone dings. The warm water washes the sweat and exhaustion off my skin. I take my soap and lather up my whole body. I'm not sure what my plan is for today but I know I don't want to be sweaty anymore. My clothes were sticking to me when I got inside. The AC drying my sweat and making it act like glue between my clothing and my skin. After that, I rub shampoo suds through my hair, making a temporary mohawk for fun. I could never rock a mohawk, and I wouldn't want to try. But even if they don't admit it, all men stand their hair straight up in the shower once in a while, just to see if they can. Once all the soap is off me, I turn off the water as the cold air of my bathroom rushes into the shower space. I climb out and grab my phone.

Brooke's name is drawn across the screen, my heart does a backflip. I read her text and my chest flutters, my stomach grows butterflies in record time. Fuck.

I was called 'girly' when I was growing up because people were scared of emotionally in tune men. I worked through it by realizing that I am just not an asshole. I mean, I am, but not like Arlo or the other people that thought I was 'too soft' to be a man. I think it's a good thing, it gives me the ability to do things differently and treat women well.

Chapter Fourteen

As I pull into the beach parking lot to meet up with Janet, Max, and Korey, I walk up to the splay of towels they are laying on. "Hey, where's Lily?" I lay down my towel next to Janet awaiting their answer. Max is on the opposite side of Janet and Korey is on Max's other side.

"She called me a little while ago, she's on her way." Janet responds, not moving from her tanning position. The boys give me hugs and say their hello's as they stand up, running towards the water to cool down. I sit next to Janet and she sits up, giving me a side hug before raising her sunglasses to the top of her head and scanning me up and down. Lowering her glasses over her eyes again she says, "I know you said y'all didn't fuck but I'm still a little disappointed there's no marks to say you lied."

"We were close." I tease, knowing she won't be able to drop the subject until she hears every last drop of tea.

She gasps and throws a hand dramatically to her chest, I give her a playful shove and roll my eyes.

"Oh whatever, you'll hear about it when we do." I wink at her and grab my sunscreen from my bag. She helps me apply it to my back as I do the rest of my body. Just as I'm putting my sunscreen away, Lily joins us and lays her towel out next to mine.

"Hey sorry guys my phone was dead when I woke up this morning." She explains as she starts taking off her shorts and shirt, putting on her own sunscreen.

"Why didn't you charge it?" I joke, helping her apply sunscreen to her back.

"I uh... Couldn't find my charger." She replies quietly, but not too quiet to be heard.

I stop rubbing in the sunscreen, "You were with Ashton?"

She turns, "What? No! What? Why would you think that?" Janet and I can tell she's lying and we exchange looks that say so.

"The girl that never lets her phone die, let her phone die. It's not that hard to guess." I shrug, turning her away from me and finishing up with the sunscreen on her back.

"Ugh whatever, yes I was with Ashton." Her face breaks out in a smile as she lays down on her towel. "We may have uh… Hooked up…" Her smile gets bigger than I thought was possible.

"*What!* No way!" Janet and I yell together. "Tell me more!" I say, begging her for all the juicy truths.

Lily spends the next several minutes talking all about her *very* late night out and the treacherous adventure to get home. Her Uber had gotten lost on the way.

"Sounds like an excellent night, I'm happy for you." Janet says. I give Lily a hug and say my congratulations. It has been a while since she seemed this happy and we were genuinely excited for her.

"Well you aren't the only one that had a great night, it seems." Janet says to Lily while giving me the sassy 'explain' eyes. Lily turns to me, confused. Once it processes that I was with Kasey her smile returns.

"Did you fuck?" She asks impatiently.

I laugh before I answer. "No, no, it was a very nice date though and he wants to go on another."

"A *date*? That's some serious stuff, girl." She eggs me on to continue explaining. I give them all the important points, including the steamy make out session in the water.

"God I'm so jealous, Max and I are great but sometimes I miss the super spontaneous stuff like making out in unconventional places." Janet groans.

"Then do something spontaneous." I say as the boys come back to their towels. Lily and them say hi and the conversations carry for a while about random things.

At some point, Korey groans about being hungry and we choose to pack up and go to Blazer's for some delicious bar food and well deserved drinks.

Walking to the cars, we decide to run to our houses and change, meet at Max and Janet's and then walk to Blazer's from there. Plans to get too drunk to drive went unsaid. But hey, at least we were safe.

Max had shots already poured for us when each of us walked into the apartment. He greeted us at the door individually and wouldn't let us fully enter until the shot was gone. I love Max, he's a party guy and I can respect it. He's the liquor that holds us together, is that how the saying goes?

I was the last to show, it took me a long time to pick my outfit in case we ran into Kasey. We hadn't talked much today but that's alright it didn't change the fact that he was running through my mind all day. I decided on a pair of black shorts and an off-white almost pink tank top. Paired with, of course, my Converse. I throw back my Tequila with the usual ritual of salt before and lime after, untie my shoes, and plop myself on the couch between Janet and Lily. They seem already pretty tipsy, giggling at random things, which meant I had some catching up to do.

"Max! I need more! I gotta get on the level of these here giggly girls!" I call to Max, knowing he will deliver. He brings me a plate of all things, with three limes, three shots of Tequila, and a pile of salt. Everything I need to get to their level.

I shamelessly gulp each one down with only a few moments between them. Waiting for it to settle in my stomach, I unlock my phone and send a text to Kasey.

"thinking about you, is that bad?"

God I wasn't even drunk yet and I'm already sending questionable texts. Makes me wonder what the rest of the night would look like. Both written and spoken.

Korey sits next to me on the couch and puts an arm around my shoulder, leaning into me. I allow it and lean into him.

"How are you doing, girly?" He asks, with a straight face so I know he wants the truth.

"I'm doing pretty good, honestly. Stressed about summer ending as always."

He sighs, "No stressing about the future bitch. You know better. Not to mention we have a few weeks." I sigh back and agree.

Lily jumps up and does a little dance to the music playing through Alexa. "You guys ready to get fucked up at Blazer's?"

She's definitely ready.

It's hot outside as we walk to Blazer's, not windy at all and no cloud in sight. The alcohol I had back at the apartment is definitely starting to set in. Making my feet feel a little fuzzy as shivers dance across my skin.

My phone buzzes in my back pocket and I reach to grab it, but get distracted by a car screeching to a halt at the stop sign 50 feet in front of us. We all pause, obviously a little traumatized from hearing the car accident outside of

Ashton's. After a few seconds, the car continues down the road normally. I laugh to break the tension.

When we walk into Blazer's there's a decent sized crowd but nothing we can't manage. Tilly has our drinks ready when we walk up to the bar, another reason we love her.

"How are my faves doing tonight?" She asks, trying to be louder than the music.

"Great! You?" We all yell back to her.

"Not too bad! Have fun guys!" She quickly returns to work tackling the line of people that have accumulated behind us to get drinks.

We start the outing on the patio since the games are full, but not before Korey calls the next round for a game of darts. Sitting in our usual seats, we begin drinking and talking.

"Let's do a mental check in." Janet says to all of us, "I just want to make sure all my people are doing good." She smiles and looks each of us in the eyes. "I'll start. I'm doing alright but groceries are expensive."

I go next, "I'm doing good but had a weird bout of grief over my mom the other day which was odd because I hardly knew her."

Max takes a breath. "I'm good and groceries are expensive." He laughs, "But seriously, I am doing good. I was missing my dad the other day, but I feel a little better now."

Next is Lily. "I've got enough of my meds to last for a while in case the doctor doesn't want to see me in time to get a refill so I'm good. But at the same time, I need medication so that sucks."

Last to speak is Korey. He looks around the patio at nothing in particular before he finally says something. "I think I am actually the happiest I've ever been before. And you guys are to thank for that."

We all gave 'awws' and fake tears, happy that Korey opened up to us that much. He was historically a closed off person, though he can open up with us, it doesn't happen very frequently.

"Thank you guys for participating, as silly as it seems. I care about you guys." Janet says before switching the vibes to stop the night from getting too sappy. Someone comes out from inside Blazer's and finds Korey, letting him know the dart board is available. We trail behind Korey, conga line style, to go play a few games of darts.

After an hour of darts and another drink, I suddenly remember that borderline embarrassing text I sent to Kasey earlier. I also remember I got a text but never checked it. I pick my phone up hoping it was Kasey that texted me.

"Not at all, I'm thinking about you too."

And a second text, **"Can I see you soon?"**

My heart flutters. I don't want to leave my friends but I do want to see Kasey. It probably wouldn't be the smartest to show up when I'm drunk. I text him back.

"how about tomorrow?"

Lily and Janet walk up to the table with another round of drinks. I definitely can't see him tonight.

"Yes please" He replies after a minute.

Chapter Fifteen

I wake up to a phone call, my phone vibrating violently, disturbing my throbbing head. I slowly sit up and grab the bottle next to me, letting my phone go to voicemail while I indulge myself in the crisp water.

I check to see who was calling and notice it is already two in the afternoon. I was out very late last night and don't remember the walk home at all. There are three text messages on my phone in addition to the missed call and a few Instagram notifications.

"You mke it home okey?" A drunk text from Lily.

"i walked you home, have a good night :) " From Korey. A small smile comes across my face.

"What would you like to do today?" The words from Kasey make my smile grow so wide my cheeks hurt.

The missed call was from Janet, the voicemail she left was a basic check in asking if I wanted to go out. I make a mental note to text her saying I have plans.

I slowly stand from my bed and walk to the bathroom. While in the shower, I rummage through the faded memories of last night, deciding what I need to patch and what is okay to leave blank. Ultimately, I don't really care one way or another.

Stepping out of the shower with my headache still in full swing, I take some Ibuprofen and get dressed in comfortable clothes, walking to the kitchen and making some coffee and toast. That is likely all I will be able to stomach.

I reach for my phone on the counter and begin to text Janet.

"i've got plans today i think, but i'll let you know" I send.

Then I open the text thread with Kasey, surprised and pleased there are no further embarrassing texts I may have drunkenly sent.

"it's up to you, maybe beach and drinks?" I click send on the message, shipping it off to Kasey's phone in an instant regardless of where he is. Grabbing my plate with buttered toast and my cup of coffee, I take a seat at the table and begin to eat while I scroll aimlessly through my phone.

My phone vibrates with a text from Kasey.

"Sounds perfect to me. I'll pick you up in an hour :) "

I stand and bring my dishes to the sink, rinsing them and placing them in the appropriate spots in the dishwasher. Returning to my room, I begin the process of getting ready.

While flipping through my clothes, my mind begins to wander to all sorts of different places. Sometimes my thoughts get the best of me, especially when the traumas start to creep back in. Today's thoughts were rash and unexpected, though.

Racing through all the times Don would hurt me and how it affected me so greatly. I was most definitely hypersexual as a result of his abuse. However, it wasn't constant. I go through phases of wanting nothing less than mind numbing and meaningless sex, and the polar opposite. Wanting no one to touch me or glance at me for longer than socially acceptable before it seems they are showing interest.

Back then, there would be a slight creak in my bedroom door when it would open. Don fixed that when he realized I was something he wanted in the most inappropriate way. He fixed it so he could enter my room silently, without me or anyone noticing.

I would only know he opened the door because of the slight change in the scent of the air or the small breeze creeping in with him. I'd pretend to be asleep for as long as I could, hoping it would deter him. But I quickly learned, he didn't care.

At first, it only happened when my aunt wasn't home. I would fight and kick and yell and try my hardest to make him stop. He would have scratches on his arms and bruises on his chest. Slowly I realized it wouldn't stop him so I gave that up. Once he recognized I wouldn't make a sound, he became more relaxed and would take advantage of me even when my aunt was home. Usually at night. This made it hard to sleep, I was always on guard. The way his teeth would sink into my skin made my stomach flip, wanting to release whatever I had eaten for dinner, but it never did.

When it finally stopped and he was gone, it took me a long time to be able to feel safe and comfortable again. As well as help from several different therapists. I had finally 'graduated' from therapy when I left for college a few years later.

I didn't jump into hypersexuality until my second year in college when I finally felt comfortable opening myself up for someone, even if it wasn't emotionally. Once I started though, the spiral began. There were lots of late nights, later than now, with extremely unsafe sex happening whenever I could get it. That doesn't help my confidence even in the slightest. Women with a higher number of sexual partners were sluts in society. Shameful.

But then came the phases. You were called worse things when you wouldn't allow someone to have you. I just couldn't stand to be touched sometimes. Certain actions or words or sounds would make me picture the awful things that happened to me growing up.

Since then I have worked through more of my trauma and don't get me wrong, I still have some struggles, but I am *significantly* better now.

My phone signals a text and my thoughts are interrupted, planting me back in current times.

"I'll be there in 10 :) " My heart races as I read the text from Kasey. Excitement and anxiety rushing through my body from my brain to my toes. I double tap his text and give a 'heart' reaction.

I finish my makeup and put on my slippers, grabbing my purse as he pulls up in the driveway waiting for me. He's standing outside his car at the passenger door when I walk up to it. He opens the door and before I have a second to step by him and climb in, he pulls me in with one arm around my waist and one hand slightly behind my head. I look up into his eyes as his lips crash into mine, causing all my racing thoughts to be washed away and I feel my body relax at his gentle touch.

"How are you, beautiful?" His words drift into my ears, smooth and fresh. I back away and slide into the seat of his car before I respond.

"Better now, how are you?" He holds up a finger and closes the door, walking around the front to his side. As he passes, I can't help but stare at him through the windshield. His white t-shirt hugging his muscular body, the tattoos peaking through the sleeves as well as the fuzzy black marks I can see *through* the white shirt, giving me a tease about the tattoos it is trying to hide. Opening his door and sitting down, he starts his car.

"I am wonderful now that you're here." He says as he backs out of my driveway and heads towards the beach.

In the water we watch the birds fly above us in the sky and the large, and small, groups of people on the beach, in the water and in between.

"What is your favorite part of California?" I ask, not only to break the comfortable silence, but also to learn more about him. I want to know everything I can about Kasey.

"The sunsets. Without a doubt in my mind." He smiles and looks at the skyline. It's not quite sunset as it's barely after three, but in just a few hours the sky will change colors every few minutes as the sun goes to sleep for the night.

"What's your least favorite thing about California?" I question him again.

"The traffic in the city. Also without a doubt in my mind."

I laugh at his answer, "Agreed on both." I smile and slowly swim just a little closer to him, missing the heat from his body the last time we were in the water together.

"What is your favorite thing about your childhood?" He asks, moving closer to me. I can tell he is nervous about asking the more serious questions, I don't really blame him.

I turn to him, "Being brought to California."

He quickly responds, "And your least favorite?" There's fear lining his voice. He knows I have had some issues in the past. Just vaguely that my uncle was arrested some years ago and I live with my aunt, but doesn't know about my parents.

"Being brought to California." I chuckle trying to hide the sadness in my voice. It's true. I do love that I was brought here, I get to enjoy the sunshine and the heat and the ocean and the good community. But I also hate that I was brought here because of all the things that happened to me when I moved here. It was a love-hate relationship.

He matches my laugh as I nod towards the beach, silently communicating that we should go lay out in the sun while it's out.

Laying on our beach towels, still wet with salt water, he continues our talk. "I'm sorry you've gone through some shit. I don't know much about it and if you don't want to talk about it with me that's okay. Just please know that I am here for you." He says as he kisses my forehead. Placing his hand on my thigh he looks out over the water and sky, which is beginning to darken as the sun slowly falls to the horizon.

"I appreciate that, Kasey. Maybe someday." I respond, trying to keep my voice sounding calm. But in reality my face feels hot and the skin under his hand feels like it is melting away and being replaced at the same time.

We sat like this for a while until Lily called me, begging me to come to Blazer's with the group. After Kasey said he was more than happy to, I told Lily we'd be there soon. She squealed in excitement. We pick up our things and get into his car, heading towards my house so I could change while he ran home and did the same.

Chapter Sixteen

I chose to wear one of my favorite cute-but-casual outfits tonight. I want to make Kasey drool but I don't want it to be obvious that I'm trying. I decide on a pair of light washed jean shorts and a low cut green tank top that shows my belly button piercing with an off-white short sleeved cardigan-type sweater, but it's more like an unbuttoned crop top. To finish off it I wore my Converse.

Kasey texts me letting me know he's out front and I grab my purse, hug my aunt goodbye, and run out the front door. Eager to be in his presence even though it's only been 30 minutes.

As I approach his car, he steps out and walks around to the passenger side, opening the door for me while planting a soft kiss on my lips. I blush and sit down, buckling my seatbelt as he walks around and gets in his own seat.

Pulling into Blazer's we find my group standing by Janet's car with an open spot next to it. Kasey takes that spot and we climb out of the car. I hug Janet and Lily while Kasey says his friendly hello's to the boys. We switch places to continue our greets and then walk inside as a group.

It is incredibly busy tonight. Busier than we are used to. Max offers to order our drinks and meet us at the table to lessen the visual stress for Tilly, Kasey goes with him. Janet, Lily, Korey and I find a table in the corner of the bar farthest from the games. Sitting around the table Korey and Lily begin pestering me with questions.

"So, what's going on with you two anyway?" Korey asks me, nodding his head in the direction of Kasey as if I wouldn't know who he was talking about.

"They're new found lovers, don't you know?" Lily teases me, nugging into my shoulder making me rock side to side.

Janet chimes in, "I'm just waiting for Brooke to tell me they finally fucked."

I laugh at that one. Janet always wants to know the nitty gritty, and I love that I always feel comfortable sharing the juicy details with her.

"We're just… Testing the waters I guess you could say." I look towards Kasey and feel my heart speed up when I notice he is looking at me. "But I'm really hoping the waters are good."

Kasey and Max come to the table with hands full of drinks. A beer for Korey, a Vodka Redbull for Lily, two Honey Traps, one for Janet and one for me, an Old Fashioned for Kasey, and a Jack and Coke for Max. Followed by Tilly bringing a tray of shots for all six of us. This was going to be a *night*.

Janet demands another check in and we all take turns and take our shot of Tequila.

Korey goes first, "I'm doing good, happy to be with my friends."

Then it follows around the table with Max next, "Same as before, doing great but groceries are expensive."

Janet is next, "I'm excited for tonight and love to see Brooklyn happy." She smiles at me and gives me a small wink just before throwing back her shot, finishing with a sour face.

"Medication is working well and it doesn't fuck me up as much when I drink so I'm great!" Lily shouts in excitement. She has tried quite a few medications and most don't mix well with alcohol, thankfully this one she's been on for a few weeks seems to be doing well for her.

Kasey, sitting next to me, goes next. "I am grateful y'all included me tonight." He takes his shot and then places

113

his hand on my thigh. Butterflies grow in my stomach and my cheeks get warm. I take a drink of my Honey Trap to blame the redness on that.

I finish the check in, "I am happy I get to be around all of you, I'm doing better lately and you guys are to thank for that." I hold my shot up towards everyone individually and then lick the salt, feeling the burning Tequila glide down my throat followed by the sour lime clenched between my teeth.

Lily stands up wanting to go to the bathroom. Janet stands with her and motions for me to join them. As I begin to stand up I realize how badly I do in fact have to pee. We are now several drinks in. Or at least us girls are. I haven't kept track of the boys' intake.

"You boys be safe, you'll end up being our rides." Janet says as we begin what feels like a treacherous adventure to the bathroom. When I stand, I see Kasey push his almost-finished drink away and stand up but I'm brisked away before I can see where he's headed.

In the bathroom, Lily yells drunkenly that she needs some toilet paper. Typical for little dive bars to run out of toilet paper. Typical for a drunk woman to not notice until she has already peed. I grab a wad from my dispenser and pass it under the wall of the bathroom stall to the one next to me.

"So what are you and Kasey's plans for the rest of the night?" Janet slurs while washing her hands in the rusty sink.

"We haven't really talked about it yet." I say, buttoning my shorts and coming out of the stall, joining Janet at the sink.

"Probably something good." Lily says, emerging from the stall with mascara beginning to rub onto her under eyes. I take a wet paper towel and wipe off the smudge. Janet laughs and I give a chuckle.

I'm nervous about the rest of the night, honestly. Kasey and I haven't really talked about boundaries. Not that I can see myself having any with him. But it would be slutty if I just handed myself to him on a platter. Not that I would particularly mind giving him that control.

Sitting back down at the table, I notice we now all have a full glass of water in front of us in addition to our alcoholic beverages. Minus Kasey's half empty water. He looks at me, smiles, and moves his mouth closer to my ear so I can hear better over the noise of the bar. "This is my second water. I'll be good, baby."

Hearing those words made goosebumps reach my feet. This man had a hold on me and I've been in denial about it. I lean my head onto his shoulder next to me and drink some of the cold water he brought over. "Thank you." I say to him as I give my liver and taste buds a break from the poison I've been feeding them the last few hours.

"You guys want to go outside?" Korey asks. I immediately stand up, stumbling over myself slightly, eager and desperate for some fresh air away from the humidity and stale air inside. Everyone stands to follow Korey and I to the patio, but not before Kasey grabs my hand to steady me and keeps it in his until we are seated again outside.

I'm not plastered at this point, but I do feel loose. If that's the right word to explain it. Part of me wants to sit here and drink three gallons of water to sober up and part of me wants to leave as soon as possible so I can let Kasey have his way with me.

We all decide to get some food. There is nothing better to soak up alcohol than greasy bar food. It is *also* true that nothing tastes better when you're drunk than greasy bar food. Lily and Janet take another trip to the bathroom and I am left with Max, Korey, and Kasey. The boys are tied up with their own conversation while I am left to stew in my thoughts. My less than hammered but still not sober thoughts. I want to finally know what it feels like to have Kasey. After all these failed attempts, it's only increasing the desire I have to feel his hands trace my breasts and his lips travel down my stomach.

I lean my head towards Kasey's and whisper, low enough that only he can hear it, "Take me home?" I say with a questioning tone, yet not asking a question. He looks at me with slight confusion so I lean back in to clarify for him, "Your home," giving him a smirk and rubbing his upper thigh, expanding on my thoughts. My very not appropriate thoughts.

He nods quickly, understanding exactly what I am asking. "Let's say goodbye to your friends and then I'll take care of you." His voice is butter. The words sliding off his tongue with a devilish look in his eyes. His right hand finds my thigh and grips it, squeezing with almost enough force to leave a bruise I wouldn't mind having.

Lily and Janet return to their food when I tell them I'm tired and want to leave.

"No you can't leave yet!" Lily protests.

"One more shot?" Janet offers, knowing if I say yes to one more I'll stay for three.

"Nah, not tonight guys. I'll see you tomorrow?" I reply, standing and saying my goodbyes.

"Ugh fine." Janet said sadly, with failed instigation in her eyes.

"See you tomorrow!" Max and Korey say together, quickly continuing their conversation we so *rudely* interrupted.

"Have a good night! Let someone know when you're home!" Lily says to me before digging into her food.

Kasey places a hand on my lower back and walks me to the front door. But not before stopping by the bar and paying off his and my tab. He offers me one more glass of water and I shake my head, "I'm alright, thank you though." His hand finds my waist and we walk through the door, climbing into his car.

The moment the door is shut I lean over to him and place my hand around the back of his head, pulling him closer to me. One of his hands does the same while the other caresses my cheek, sending chills through my body. His soft lips meet mine and his tongue teases me, requesting to fill me with warmth. My tongue dances with his and I feel his breath get heavy. I have never felt so much urge. I have never felt someone want me in this much of an intimate way with such care and kindness.

My brain spins, but not because of the alcohol. It spins because of excitement.

Chapter Seventeen

The ride to Kasey's isn't very long. He lives with two other roommates in a three bedroom, two bathroom condo that is surprisingly spacious and clean. We take off our shoes at the front door and walk up two flights of stairs. His room is at the top of the house on the third floor, and thankfully, this is the only room on that floor along with a bathroom.

Kasey's room is a good size. A queen bed tucked against a light blue wall with two side tables, a desk and a dresser along the other wall. Light blue paint also covers the one with the window and some soft orange lamps in two of the corners. The bathroom is attached but has a door to separate the two spaces, with a stand up shower and a black top sink, which I had never seen before but instantly fell in love with.

As he walks into the room behind me he closes the door and turns off one of the lamps, allowing a calm amount of light to shine through the room. I watch him walk up to his desk and set his phone on the charger, smiling at the little detail of following what I can only assume is his routine. He catches me smiling, "What's that for?" He takes a few steps towards me and cocks his head to the side, pressing the question with inaudible clues.

"Nothing, you're just cute." I say breaking eye contact and browsing the rest of the details in his room. His bed has a gray comforter and black pillow cases, shockingly more than two pillows. Immediately earning him some extra points.

"*Just* cute?" He gives a playful frown, "I was hoping for a little more than that." He wraps a hand around my waist and pulls me closer suddenly. A breath escapes my lungs and I feel myself melt to his touch.

"You are… Incredible." I say before I can process the words falling out of my mouth, his free hand finding the curve of my neck, tilting my face to meet his.

"It's a little too soon to be saying that now, Brooklyn." He says, the sound of my name has a rasp to it as it falls off his lips sending shivers down my spine, goosebumps on my arms and legs, and yet another breath to escape my mouth, which is just an inch from his. His body presses against mine and the force of it makes me trip a step backwards towards his bed. Giggling, he catches me and then slowly lays me down onto his comfortable mattress, not gaining any space between our bodies. I can feel him hardened in his pants against my lap when his lips crash into mine. His tongue dancing across my lips as I allow them to part. My hand finds the back of his head and I grab some of his hair, not hard, but just hard enough to squeeze a faint gasp out of his lungs. He pushes himself into me more.

Minutes into a very heated session, he stands up, causing my whole body to shiver missing his warmth. He rips off his shirt and tosses it across the room next to the bathroom, he has this sense of desire like he wants to eat me whole. This sense of animalistic craving that I find so attractive.

Without him needing to ask, I slide my shirt up over my head, throw it in the same direction as his, and look up at him standing at the edge of the bed. My eyes are laced with Tequila, impatience, and all encompassing lust. He must be able to read them because he slides his pants down, keeping his boxers on and climbs back over me, reaching an arm around my back and undoing my bra with one hand, removing it with the other, and dropping it at his side. Once his hand is free, he takes one and wraps it lightly around my neck, pausing for consent.

My brain is overwhelmed. But in a really good way. I think? I want this, I want this so badly. The tension that has been building up is incredibly too large for me to handle without letting loose and giving in to him. But there's something stopping me. Something hard to single out, but also too large to miss.

The way Kasey makes me feel is something I have never felt before. Don't get me wrong, I have felt good things with different connections and relationships, but something is distinctly more intimate with Kasey. And the fact that we haven't even fucked yet but I still felt this connected was odd to me. Not in a bad way, just in a new way.

I think I have worked so hard to protect myself ever since things got bad with Don, that it's been hard to know when I can put my walls down. Instantly when getting to know Kasey I knew that with him, I would have the ability to let them down, and it would be worth it. Of course it would take some time, but I could tell it was possible.

Kasey can sense my hesitation and removes his gently placed hand, breaking the connection between us. I see his soft eyes look me over, trying to read what I'm feeling. After a few seconds of him deciphering my mood, he speaks, "Are you okay?" His voice is filled with concern, as are his eyes.

"Yeah, sorry. I'm okay." I respond as he backs away more, sitting on the edge of his bed, still close enough to share our warmth, but far enough to give comfortable distance.

"Don't apologize, do you need anything?" He asks and starts to stand, "Your shirt? My shirt? Water? A ride home?"

I grab his arm before he steps away from the bed and out of reach, "No, I'm okay, I promise. Sometimes my head just races in the worst moments." I shake my head and look down in my lap, now sitting criss-crossed with one of his pillows covering my breasts. He grabs for a shirt anyway, handing me the one he took off himself just a little while ago. I slip it over my head and look back to him, my hair peeking out of the neck of the shirt.

He sits next to me on the bed and slowly reaches an arm out towards me. He searches my face for an answer before continuing. Grabbing my hair gently from the shirt and resting it on my shoulders and back he looks at me, "Talk to me?"

Part of me is shocked he isn't mad that I ruined what was supposed to be a perfect first night together. Don't get me wrong, I'm glad he isn't freaking out but at the same time, it's almost strange he isn't. So many men in my past have gotten mad or disappointed or frustrated if I don't put out when it comes down to it. But they don't understand, sometimes you just get subconsciously *triggered* out of nowhere. And there really isn't a ton that you can do for that. My heart's mostly healed, but my body still remembers.

I mean sure, you've got your techniques and your support systems and your coping skills. But those are for after you get triggered. It's hard to fight the pre-triggering because you never really know what's going to do it. I wouldn't even go as far as to say I am triggered right now, maybe just some anxiety. I don't know. I just wish I could explain this all to Kasey without sounding demented.

"I don't know how to speak all my thoughts and not come off as crazy." I decide to finally say, breaking the long silence between us.

"First of all, you're not crazy. You've had some not-so-great shit happen to you and none of that is your fault. You're doing what you know to do to be *better* and that makes you *not* crazy." He relaxes on one arm next to me, still close but keeping a respectful distance.

I reach out and grab his hand that isn't supporting his weight and run my thumb along the back of it. Making eye contact now, "I appreciate you trying to understand, it means a lot." I take a breath before I continue. "There's just been some... As you said... Not-so-great shit... Uhm, do we want to get into this now?"

He places his hand on my thigh and sits up a little to make sure I am seeing him. "You only need to say what you are comfortable sharing. We have all the time in the world for the rest."

Chapter Eighteen

My mind is racing on what Brooke could have gone through. Racing trying to figure out what she is hesitant to share. Whatever it is, I can understand random triggers and PTSD flashbacks. For a long while I wouldn't walk into my parents' bedroom after my mom first OD'd. I was afraid there would be something in the air that could hurt me the same way it hurt her. I know now that was an irrational fear, but it still had a hold on me until shortly before I left for college.

My heart goes out to her. For being vulnerable, even on the smallest scale. It's difficult to work through things, even if you go to therapy. It's not for everyone and if you do go, there are mounds of homework you have to do on your own because one person can't just heal you. You have to meet them halfway, maybe even farther.

My body aches for her. The tension between Brooke and I has only grown since we reconnected at Ashton's party. The other night at the beach was exhilarating. It made me crave her touch, crave her voice, crave feeling all of her. As much as I wanted this with her right now, it's not the right time.

I'm not sure what kind of support she needs right now, but I want to be the one to give it to her at this moment. I don't want to be overbearing, but I want to show her I am here. I have my fair share of childhood hardships and I want nothing more than to exchange stories about what made us who we are. I am willing to be an open book for her, answer any and all of her questions. It's up to her if she wants to be an open book with me as well, though I am biased and want her to be comfortable with me. I just have to make her comfortable, that part is up to me.

I always wondered what happened to her parents. Why did she have to stay with her aunt and uncle? I also always wondered why her uncle went to jail a while back. There were a few rumors about why when we were in school, but none of them made sense in explaining why

Brooke had such a visceral reaction to us starting to mesh into one being.

He was a coke addict that stole a car.

He beat up neighborhood dogs.

After a while it was like everyone just pretended it didn't happen. The rumors slowly died down and no one talked about it. Which is probably for the better I can imagine. Seeing as the real story was probably much worse than anyone could imagine.

She has a soft look in her eyes. The green I love so much seems a little more hazel in the lighting. Her cheeks are rosy, probably from the heated moments we shared. My ability to turn off is almost as easy as it is to turn on. I have always been *very* educated on consent. I think it is an important thing to know for anyone, but especially men. As well as non-verbal signs that someone shows when they want to stop, even if you've already started. People are allowed to say yes and change their mind. It's important to respect peoples' boundaries, and help them draw the boundaries if you can see they aren't able to but want them in place.

I could tell that Brooke wanted to stop. Or at least wanted to pause. I respected that and created space, she didn't have to ask for it. She didn't have to beg me to stop. She didn't have to force me to stop. She seems taken aback by that and it causes a tinge of pain in my chest, sadness creeps into my stomach and I can feel a burning pit growing behind it.

Arlo has never been formally accused of raping someone. But I also know he has a temper that could, *and does*, scare people sometimes. I wouldn't be surprised if he has created situations for himself in which the woman he was with regretted it after. His favorite ones to go for were drunk women. Not so drunk that they would be unconscious or passed out, but drunk enough that he seemed more attractive than he was and they were less likely to say no even if they wanted to. This, I believe, was the only reason he was able to get with so many women. I honestly think that's disgusting. Arlo is fucking disgusting.

Luckily, I am a man. Arlo is a boy. And honestly, I might kill him if he ever came *near* Brooke in any manner other than a wave from across the room. He doesn't deserve her. He doesn't deserve to know more than her name. And to make sure that is never a possibility, I need to make her mine. I need to get over my fears. Maybe that's why he creeps into my skin so easily.

Anger stems from fear after all.

Chapter Nineteen

"It's hard for me to talk about, so I try not to. That time in my life is done and gone" I say to him, soft spoken. He says nothing, just gives me an encouraging look to continue at my own speed.

My phone chimes several times. I check the time as I pick it up and am shocked it's only ten o'clock.

"Brooklyn?"

"You need to come home."

"Call the police."

I drop my phone and shoot up as fast as I can. Getting dizzy as I stand from the sudden jolt of energy, my vision begins to turn black and I can't tell which way is up. Kasey sees my struggle and quickly stands and helps to steady me, as he does he says "Woah, are you okay?"

I say nothing. I find my pants and start grabbing my things. Why the fuck would my aunt tell me to call the police and rush home? Is she okay? Did someone break into the house? Did she fall down? I forget where I am and finally Kasey grabs my wrist and stops me dead in my tracks.

"Brooklyn, talk to me." He moves the hair in my face and tucks it behind my ear.

I pause, "I.. I don't know. It's my aunt."

And with this, he says no more. He throws on his clothes and we both run out of the room. I almost trip while putting on my shoes during the walk-run to his car. He starts driving the moment our asses hit the seat and we buckle. I don't speak for the first few minutes of the drive, lost in my thoughts. Fire burns in my stomach as it reaches for my throat.

Is she going to be alive when we get there? What are we walking into? Does she need an ambulance? Police. I remember she told me to call the police and I grab my phone from my purse and unlock it, dialing 911.

"9-1-1. What's the location of your emergency?" The operator on the other end of the phone asks.

"Hi, it's my aunt. I don't know what's going on but I'm on my way home and she told me to call the police." I spit out her address and the dispatcher asks more questions about her name, description, and what I think could be happening.

"I have no fucking idea! I was out and she panic-texted me telling me to call the police so I'm rushing home!" I shout back, fearful of the unknowns and frustrated at the number of questions.

"I'm sorry, ma'am. I'm just scared." I apologize to the lady that was kind enough to even answer my distress call in the first place.

She takes a breath, "It's alright ma'am, I understand the stress of the situation. Just drive safe, we will have some officers meet you there."

"Thank you so much." I say as I hang up the phone, staring out the window with my thoughts going faster than I thought was possible.

Kasey places his hand on my thigh as it bounces in his passenger seat. "Talk to me. Let's work through this. I don't want you alone in your head right now, I'm here."

I look at him while he focuses on the road and getting me to my aunt safely. His silhouette from the streetlights is a soft, possessing sight to see that warms my heart and calms my mind. I look down at his hand on my thigh, caressing my knee with his thumb ever so gently. I feel better in the last five seconds than I did in the last eight minutes.

"I honestly don't know." I snap. "I just want to get there and make sure she's alright."

He nods his head and continues to drive.

We pull into the driveway three seconds before the police come pulling up behind us in front of the sidewalk. Two cop cars with their flashing lights on angle towards our house showing they came from different directions. Creating a perfect angle like it was practiced for a movie. Ready to go.

"Stay in the car!" The four officers yell at us as they begin to approach the house. "We will scope things out to make sure it's safe."

I sit back down and close the door to Kasey's car, beginning to shake. Kasey grabs my hand, following the cops with his eyes as he reaches to put a hand on my back. I jump at his touch, having a gut feeling something shitty is happening inside that house and being surprised by someone's presence is an unsettling feeling.

For some reason, I have a sense. A sense I haven't felt in 10 years. I hear my aunt yell. Angry. Angrier than I have heard in 10 years. I hear the police shout. They shout a name I haven't heard in 10 years. One I tried so hard to forget.

Don.

I look at Kasey, with horror on my face. "You should leave. I'll call you later." I try to stay calm, realizing what's happening.

He stutters in his breath, "What? Let me stay with you to make sure you're okay." He rubs my arm and I pull away.

"Please leave. I'll call you later." I say again, not allowing an argument this time. He looks at me. Sadness, confusion, and pain lace his expression. So much of each you can hardly isolate them individually. He removes his arms from the passenger side of the car and nods.

"Please call me." He says as I open his car door and step out. I don't turn around as I slowly walk up the driveway to the open front door. I can tell he is waiting for me to turn around, but I stand my ground and he begins to drive away.

I wait by the front door, out of view, standing to the side so I can hear what's happening inside. I hear the metal clanging of handcuffs with the click of them being locked. I hear the police saying the same words they said 10 years ago.

"Don Baring, you have the right to remain silent. Anything you say can..." They say as Don begins to argue back.

"What the fuck! I'm trying to see my fucking wife!" He shouts with fury in his voice failing to mask the slur of his words. Only they divorced shortly after he went to prison, when Bev started going to AA. He's delusional. I turn the corner of the door and see two police officers in the living room with Don in cuffs, one in the kitchen, and one in the middle of the hallway. I keep scanning the room, finding my aunt sitting in the hallway behind the cop separating her and Don, nearly at the back corner. She's shaking, crying, and sweating.

I run to her side. Instantly wrapping my arms around her, caressing her head against my chest, rocking her back and forth. She looks at me and I see the rubbed mascara streaming down her round cheeks.

"He just showed up. He showed up and started pushing me around. I didn't know what to do. He... He hurt me." She shakes as she speaks. It was at this point, I noticed she didn't have a shirt on and had a bite mark on her shoulder blade. A fucking bite mark.

After my after-school snack, I ran to my bedroom. The pink walls and butterfly fairy lights strung up and blinking. When I got home I noticed there were no cars in the driveway. I was excited to read my newest book from the library, *Junie B. Jones and the Yucky Fruitcake*. I slam my bedroom door and jump onto my bed, grabbing the book from my backpack and opening to the start page.

Suddenly I hear the garage door slam shut. Fear and pain rush over my body. He's home early. I try to move something in front of my bedroom door but I'm not strong enough to move my desk or bookshelf so I have nothing. My door swings open just as I sit back down on my bed, staring at Don in the doorway.

"What are you doing?" He asks me, devious eyes piercing my eight year old ones.

"I was just reading my new book" I say, knowing why he's here but not wanting to admit it.

"You know what to do. Don't fight me this time." He growls, not giving me a chance to move. He closes and locks the door, moving towards me on the edge of my bed. When he reaches me, he smiles and slaps me across the face. The sting goes so deep I can feel it in my brain and I get a shocking headache. He throws me to lay down on the bed so hard I bounce and once my face is buried in the blanket, he sighs with disgusting desire. A single tear streaking down my face.

Incoherent shouts shake me back to the now as three of the police officers walk Don out to one of the cruisers. The last remaining one walks down the hall to my aunt and I. She looks up at him and he speaks, "Are you okay? Do you need medical care?" Tenderness in his voice, knowing the behaviors of domestic violence and how they affect everyone in the family.

She avoids my eye contact as she looks down at herself. "Yes, please" she pleads softly. He nods his head and speaks into his radio, requesting medical.

The ambulance arrives a few minutes later and they come to my aunt's side. I step back to give them room, giving her a merciful look showing my love. They begin to talk as the police officer asks to speak to me. I follow him into the kitchen.

"Do you have someplace to stay tonight?" He asks me, looking around, "This may be a crime scene here soon."

In shock, I open my mouth but close it to think. I could call any one of my friends, but they're probably either still out drinking, or too drunk to be of any help. I could call Kasey, but I don't want to bother him too much in one night. Not to mention I was kind of a bitch to him earlier.

"Yeah, I think so." I say to the cop before making up my mind. He tells me I should call them now. Now? I still don't know who the fuck I'm calling. "Okay, I'll go do that." I say to him as I walk to my room and begin to pack a bag. I'm so scrambled I grab random things that I definitely won't need. When I realize my bag is full and I have close to nothing of use, I take everything out and start again. Blue oversized sleep shirt and light pink shorts. Underwear for tonight and tomorrow. Yellow-orange bathing suit. Jean shorts and a dark purple T-shirt. Toothbrush and toothpaste.

I dial a number on my phone, after a moment of ringing, a voice answers.

"Brooklyn? Are you okay?"

Chapter Twenty

It takes me a moment to gather my thoughts into actual words. Shaking, I reply. "No. Can you come get me?" I walk outside the house to get some fresh air. And see my aunt being loaded into the ambulance on the stretcher. She looks distraught, but still calm. I know she's just trying to be strong for me.

"Yeah of course. I'm on my way." The voice says in my ear, bringing my focus back to the phone call. Unable to speak, I try to take a deep breath but it comes out in a shudder from the anxiety. "And Brooklyn? Take some deep breaths. I'll be there soon." The phone call ends as the ambulance drives away.

A few minutes later, a white Jeep pulls into the driveway next to where I've been sitting since we hung up. He gets out and quickly walks around his car, no hesitation when he sits on the cold asphalt next to me.

"Hey, B" Kasey speaks, his voice glazed with calming comfort, prepared for whatever crazy thing I could say next. To no one's surprise, I say nothing.

"Where would you like to go? My house? Hotel? Drinks? Friends? What do you need right now?" He asks, wrapping an arm around my shoulders, pulling me close enough that I feel his warmth radiate towards me but can still breathe. I shrug my shoulders, unsure of what I really need and unable to process all the options he gave me. I bury my head into his chest.

Kasey stands, "I know what you need. Stand up, pretty girl." If it weren't for the event that took place less than an hour ago, those words would have sent me into three other dimensions, instead, they sent me to two other dimensions. His ability to give me these feelings is hardly affected by difficult situations.

In the car, I stare out the window blankly, not paying attention to the route. Numb to my core and only keeping a foot in reality because of Kasey's hand on my thigh, lightly rubbing it with his thumb. I tune in on the road and notice we are turning into the beach parking lot. "What are we doing here?" I ask him hesitantly.

He doesn't reply as he parks his car and hands me the bag I packed. Turning to me and back to the relaxed ocean waters, he finally speaks. "I'm sure you packed a bathing suit, put it on and I'll wait right outside. You need some salt-water therapy."

It's a struggle to change into a bikini in the car, especially when your mind is halfway out the door. But eventually I emerge from his backseat and see him leaning against the worn, wooden fence lining the parking lot. The sky is black, a few clouds rolling across the moon moving ever so slightly. The ocean is a deep blue, making it difficult to see the threshold between sky and sea the farther out you look. The air is crisp but not cold, a perfect mix for night swimming. God this man was good.

Walking back up to Kasey's car, he speaks for the first time since we got here.

"You feeling any better?" His car unlocks as we approach it. I feel bad for not talking to him after his kind gesture tonight.

"I'm feeling much better, but still not the best." I respond back to him, being honestly vague.

He opens his passenger door, reaches in to turn on the heater and seat warmer, lays out a towel for me on the seat, and backs away allowing me to sit. Walking around the front, he looks out at the ocean and back at me. My cheeks feel warm.

As he gets in, I watch him buckle his seatbelt and begin to reverse from his parking spot. How can someone care so deeply about me, enough to bring me to my favorite spot when I need it most, when I don't even give him half the effort? How can someone want to help me when I am so unloveable? How can someone show so much interest when I am broken?

"I really appreciate you, Kasey." I finally thank him, long overdue. "Thank you for being here."

He draws in a breath, not laced with anger or irritability, but with tenderness and concern. "There is nowhere else I'd rather be," he says as he places his hand back on my thigh. "Now, where am I taking you?"

The question I was waiting for, but still don't know how to answer. I don't want to go home, there's once again bad memories that I don't want to be alone with. I don't feel safe. I don't want to go to his house, inviting myself would be rude. I don't want to call any of my friends, I'm in the tunnel mood where I want to block everything out, shut the blinds, drink myself into oblivion, lock the doors.

"Nowhere." I respond, tears lining the rims of my eyes. I shake it off and stare out the window.

Kasey pulls off the road into a side street parking spot, opening his door and without a word he walks away. Confused, I follow his steps with my eyes up to Janet's door. The door opens after a few moments, inaudible speaking between the two of them before Janet walks out with him, her favorite blanket wrapped around her shoulders. I can see distress wiped across her face. I don't know what he said to her, but she is worried. She opens my door, grabs my bag from between my feet, and starts to wrap the blanket around my half-naked body. Silently, she leads me up to her front door. I turn around just before crossing the threshold and see Kasey leaning against his car, watching to make sure we make it inside safely.

"I'm here if you need anything, one call away." He says to me as Janet and I walk inside.

Janet speaks carefully, "Are you doing alright? What happened? He just said you needed a friend." We are sitting on her couch now, I changed into shorts and a long sleeve shirt. There is a book and a half empty mug of tea on the coffee table. I ruined her comfortable evening wind-down after a day of drinking.

"I don't know," which is honest.

"Stop being vague, B. Talk to me." She begs.

The tears that have been slowly filling my vision finally spill over their thresholds and run down my cheeks, slowly at first and then uncontrollable.

"He came back." Is all I can manage to say between hushed sobs, her eyes widen, anger running through her veins.

Janet knows a good majority of my past, she kinda had to seeing as I spent a good amount of time at her house when I was younger. She saw the bite marks and bruises when I changed clothes even though I tried my best to hide them.

"Where is he?"

"The police took him again. He hurt her." I recall the bite mark I saw on Bev's shoulder. Red and dented but not quite dripping with blood like mine once would.

"He's a dead man." She says, with no further questions. Just holding me and allowing me to process what happened tonight.

I always wondered *Why me?* Why was *I* the one that suffered so much growing up? Why did he want to do those things to *me*? I tried to follow religions but they always said *God has a plan.* What kind of fucking *plan* involves grown men sexually and physically assaulting children? What kind of plan killed my parents? What kind of plan puts children through these tragedies?

That's why Beverly drank so much and why I drink so much and try to blind out the memories with weed and get tattoos to give me some form of physical pain to cover up the emotional pain. To stop the repulsive thoughts of my past. To stop the nightmares. To stop the thoughts that I was better off dead. Although, I guess it never worked really well, just a bandaid to keep me going.

Janet and I fall asleep cuddling on the couch. I wake up a few hours later to Max walking into the living room, wearing only boxers. He startles at the sight of me, not realizing I was sleeping on his couch with his girlfriend.

"Hey Brooke, sorry I didn't know you were here." He says quietly, to not wake Janet and grabs a pair of sweatpants from his room and puts them on.

"I'm sorry, I had a rough night and Kasey thought I should be here." I replied, just as softly.

"That's okay, I'm glad you're here. Better than not I'm sure. You hungry?" He offers.

"No, I'm alright."

"Too bad." He smiles and walks up to Janet, kissing her forehead. Janet lets a little groan out before stirring and ultimately stretching. Max goes into the kitchen and begins cooking eggs and bacon for the three of us.

I love my people. My guardian angels. But this is tough.

Chapter Twenty One

There isn't enough air in the world to help me between the dry heaves. My skin is cold like ice but my insides are hot like fire. The sweat beading on my forehead reeks of alcohol and mistakes. I try to sit back from the toilet long enough to think of something other than emptying myself in the bowl. I fucked up.

Yesterday, a few days after Beverly went to the hospital, I did something I thought I never would.

My bottle of Tequila, or should I say my fourth in less than a week, had run dry. Wanting more, I got into my car and headed to the gas station a few minutes away. Having a last minute thought that I should walk, I shoved it down and turned on the engine, pulling out of my driveway. It was late, late enough that I knew none of my friends would stop by to check on me and see my car was gone. My brain is fuzzy, my feet are numb, and my hands don't act as quickly as my brain tells them too.

I forget to unbuckle before trying to get out of my car. The fabric cuts into the side of my neck and causes a burn. A mix between a rug burn and a paper cut. I groan and unbuckle, attempting to get out of my car the second time was more successful.

I grab the largest bottle of liquor I can carry, a bag of chips, and a bottle of OJ. Setting them on the counter, the clerk takes one look at me before ringing up my items and telling me my total. I know he can see my red eyes, disheveled hair, makeup-streaked under eyes, and he can probably smell the Tequila like I can. I slide my card, grab my things, and head out the door.

Driving through town this late at night, when I shouldn't be, is an interesting feeling. The wind is subtle against my car but I can see it stronger in the trees. The street lights showing me the barrier between road and sidewalk didn't help me any.

Suddenly, my car jolts and I am confused. Unaware of where exactly I am for the first few minutes, I look around. I am three blocks past my house, half on the sidewalk, my car's front end kissing a tree. I wasn't going very fast, but I still made it over the curb. My heart starts beating faster, my head straightens out after a quick shake, and the truth of what happened lingers above me.

I back my car off the curb, to a spot where it seems I was just parking intentionally, and get out to assess the damage.

Luckily, the tree had nothing but a missing piece of bark. Those resilient fuckin' trees. My car on the other hand, relatively okay given the circumstances. The plastic grill had cracked and the fender popped out of its home. I walked up to it and kicked the fender back into place, climbed back in my car, and continued home to truly process this mistake.

Keeping as calm as I could, I stepped out of my car, noticing the silence around me. The damage to my front end truly wasn't too bad. Not noticeable unless you look closely or know what happened.

This is where the shock sets in.

Now I sit in the corner of my room. Bottle of OJ in one hand, bottle of liquor in the other. I take a swig of each, struggling to swallow. My mind begins to race and I can't help the thoughts.

> *I could have died.*
> *I could have killed someone.*
> *That was fucking stupid.*
> *Why wouldn't I just walk?*
> *That could have been so much worse.*

It doesn't stop there. With how much I've drank at this point since I got home, I'm surprised my brain is even coherent enough to form thoughts.

My friends are going to kill me.

Beverly is going to kill me.

I could have ended up like Charlotte.

That right there. That was the kicker. I had never driven drunk before and I don't know why my subconscious thought today was the perfect day for it. My body took over before my brain could give a reasonable excuse to walk. Before finishing the thought that would have stopped this from happening in the first place.

What would I have done if my car had lost the fight against the tree? What would Janet have done? Lily? Max? Korey? Beverly? Kasey? What would they have thought? Would they think I did it on purpose? A passive successful suicide? A purposeful successive suicide? Would they have healed from it?

There were so many thoughts I couldn't keep them straight. I felt guilty, thankful, angry. So many feelings and so many thoughts I didn't know how to handle.

Pause. You know how to deal with these things. You were taught in therapy.

Breathe.

Look around and find five things you can see. Bed frame, closet door, carpet, picture of my closest friends and I on the dresser, water bottle on night stand.

My breathing slows.

Look around and find four things you could hear. Fan humming on the ceiling, ocean winds rustling trees outside my open window, dishwasher in the kitchen rattling with water, clock ticking seconds in the hallway.

Look around and find three things you can feel. Carpet fibers scratching at the backs of my legs, the cold bottle of orange juice in my hand, the hard wall against my back.

I'm starting to feel better.

Look around and find two things you can smell. The candle I lit is finally emitting the smell of gardenias and lemon grass, the smell of my unwashed hair.

My legs stop trembling.

Look around and find one thing you can taste. Tears.

I wipe my eyes, set down the bottles I was double-fisting, and stand up. I turn the lamp on my nightstand on and leave my bathroom door open as I take a shower. This won't fix the migraine I'll have in the morning but at least I won't smell like death.

I could have died.

I could have killed someone.

Stop, everything is fine. The only people that will know are the people you tell.

Who am I going to tell?

I restart my grounding technique in the shower. I had used this way of calming myself down a number of times, only a number I could count on two hands. I never thought it worked for me, but maybe I wasn't *letting* it help. Because now, it was working wonders.

I need to spend my days doing more than drinking away my sorrows. Beverly isn't dead, I'm not dead, my friends aren't dead. Let's keep it that way. I cleaned the whole house and made it a bit of a game to see how long I could keep it looking un-lived in. I did pretty well, even though I continued to drink. Just more controlled, safer, and never first thing in the morning like I had been before.

Chapter Twenty Two

Alcohol has been helping me. I'm not going absolutely crazy, but I'm not taking it easy either. I'm still going on runs every morning, sometimes every other morning. But my head has been in a strange place. A place filled with anxiety, fear, a small amount of anger, and heartache.

The last week and a half have been slightly blurred. I went to a few parties and got too drunk for comfort. Walking there and back to make sure I was safe. I kept my ringer turned all the way up at all times just in case I was needed. Only hoping for one person's text.

It's difficult to get so close to someone over a period of time and then have it ripped away from you over something you don't fully understand.

I haven't seen or heard from Brooke in just as long and it's been killing me. My mind is full of worry but I'm not sure how to help her. I don't know hardly anything about what happened that night and it scares me. I don't like being scared. Looking through our messages, I notice she still hasn't read my text. I decide to text Ashton to see if he knows anything.

"You still messing around with Lily?" I send, thinking that if he is I can get some information from him.

Waiting for a text, I get up and take a few hits off the joint I have sitting on my desk from the other night. I hop in the shower, skipping my run for the day.

My phone pings after I dry off and get dressed.

"yeah bro she's great" Ashton said.

"Any chance you know anything about Brooke from her?" I reply, desperate for *something*.

I don't want to blow up Brooke's phone and annoy her with texts I'm sure she wouldn't want to deal with, and I'm sure someone in her friend group knows something. I just want to know that she's okay. At minimum, I need to know she's breathing.

My stomach growls at me, I've been eating like shit because I have been so worried. Sleeping like shit, too. Still wrapped in the towel from my shower, I walk down the flight of stairs that lands me in the kitchen. I grab a bowl and pour some Cheerios into it, topping it off with milk. After grabbing a spoon, I sit at the table and doom scroll while I eat my sad, boring breakfast.

I remember when I was younger, Cheerios were my favorite cereal. They are so bland to me now I'm not sure why I loved them so much. I'm sure it had something to do with the fact that I could eat it easily whenever I wanted without worrying about bothering my always-busy-with-something parents.

"Sorta, she's been MIA from everyone lately but it sounds like it was something to do with her uncle. I'm sure she's okay, man. Lily said Janet was tryin to call her a bit ago."

The next text to come through is from a number I don't recognize.

"if i get B to answer will u pick her up? -Janet"

I text back immediately, "Yes"

Once I save Janet's number in my phone, I put my now empty bowl in the dishwasher and climb the stairs to my room as my phone rings.

"Hey" Janet says through the speaker.

"Hey what's going on?" I ask, closing my bedroom door.

"I got her to answer, beach day?" She says, I can tell she is proud of herself for getting through to Brooke.

"Oh thank God, how did she seem?" I scramble through my drawers to find something quick to put on. I settle on black swim trunks and a dark red T-shirt. My brain starts to put the pieces together on what happened with

Brooke last time I saw her, but there are too many missing details for it to make complete sense to me.

"She seems... Okay? I don't know, it's hard to tell. Want to go pick her up?"

"Yes please, when?" I eagerly say, grabbing my keys off my dresser.

"Right now if you can!" She says enthusiastically.

"On my way!" I say and hang up the phone, sliding it into my shorts pocket. I slip on my white shoes and grab a water bottle from the fridge. An elated grin spreads across my face at the thought of being at the beach with Brooke again. I start to slip into rated R thoughts of what would have happened but quickly reel myself back into present times. I've got to get my girl.

I climb into the driver's seat of my car, turning the keys, and reversing out of the driveway. My mind travels far and wide on the way to her house. I am so excited to see Brooke. I can't wait to feel her lips against mine and feel her body in my arms. The time without her has been weird. We have only seen each other a little, but not being around her feels wrong inside.

I need her.

Chapter Twenty Three

I roll over in bed, surrounded by sunlight piercing my eyes. As the light forces my eyes open I see the main reason I'm feeling this way sitting on my nightstand directly next to me. It practically makes me sick just looking at the clear glass bottle missing a large amount of the Tequila that once lived in it. Knowing it's now in my body causes goosebumps to grow across my skin and a dry heave to escape from my gut.

I run my hands over the fluffy comforter I'd just had a rock-hard sleep under and find my plastic water bottle and cell phone. Opening the water, I sit up in bed and unlock my phone while chugging the rest of the water.

"where u at?" One of Lily's messages says.

"are you okay???" From Janet.

"come in come in" Max sent a few days ago.

"I'm worried about you, Brooke.." Kasey had said.

"HEY. EARTH TO BROOKE." Another one from Max.

As well as several other missed texts and calls stacked up in my notification center. Not to mention the tens of Instagram reels from Janet. Voicemails begging me to answer the font door. All their attempts failed. I needed time.

Time for the morning-after routine. Brush teeth. Shower, water hot. Wash face. Soap hair. Wash body. Contemplate life. Dry off. Try not to pass out in the process.

Getting ready for the day is a slow process due to the fact that I smoked weed fresh out of the shower. Sitting next to my open window, even though I'm home alone and have been for almost two weeks. I spark up the joint I bought a few days ago preparing for a morning like this.

I grab my black jean shorts and sunflower yellow tank top, and get dressed at half-speed for nothing in particular and don't even mind. Not sure what else I would do with my time besides this. At the very least, getting up and 'ready' for the day made me feel like I still had something to do. Made me feel productive. Even if I spent the rest of the day drinking and smoking to hide the fear. I don't want to be angry, and anger stems from fear, so I have to avoid the fear. Right? Right.

The time I have in the 'morning' before speaking to another human is sacred for me. I had so little of those moments when I was younger. Whenever I was alone for more than 20 minutes I got nervous something was going to happen to me. And more often than not, I was right. It was like Don had a radar for when I was 'available' to him.

I'd be begging him to stop before he even walked into my room. Before he even closed the door and locked in on me. Before he would even touch me.

After he was finished, the very first thing I would do was cry. For the first few years that is. Once I cried out all my tears over the same thing for long enough, my emotions died out. My systems shut down. The only thing that kept me alive was alone time *outside* of the house. He couldn't touch me outside of the house. Too many potential witnesses.

In the last few weeks there has been a lot of… Coping. I have not spoken to anyone, have not seen a single soul, and Bev is still not home. She's been in the hospital since the night Don came back and took his anger out on her since I wasn't there to receive it. I blame myself for it. If I would have been home she wouldn't have gotten hurt the way I used to.

After her original visit to the hospital on that night, she was discharged and sent home. The night I was at Janet and Max's, she came home to an empty house and found all the liquor and medications she could.

Tylenol.
Benadryl.
Oxycodone.
Escitalopram.
Ibuprofen.
Xanax.

With all the medication she had on standby, sitting alone in her bathtub, water running through the shower spout above her, she washed away the pills one handful at a time. Followed by the half bottle of Vodka I had hidden in my closet.

Alone, she cried. She wailed. She recognized what she had done and regretted it quickly. Calling 911 on herself, the police showed up confused as to why they were returning to this address so soon.

Once at the hospital for the second time in 12 hours, she lost consciousness from everything she had taken, the poisons finally taking hold of her body. The doctors were rushing around, nurses doing everything they could to reverse the actions Beverly took to put herself in this urgent situation.

I woke up to a call from the hospital and rushed to visit her the next morning, once she was awake and stable. Luckily, the emergency room was able to save her life without any major complications. We spoke for as long as they would allow visitors and she had decided to switch to inpatient treatment. She wants to get better. And those were the best words she'd ever said to me.

She told me she regretted her decisions because she didn't want to leave me. *Me*. I was the reason she wanted to stay.

"I never realized how truly horrible he was to you. When I got a taste of it... I..." She takes a deep breath. Sitting in the hospital bed with it slightly perked up just so she could look at me.

The oxygen tubing resting on her cheeks reaching her nose and tucked behind her ears, she looks me in the eyes. Reaching for my hand, I can feel the steel-cold fingers that barely belong to her grab mine.

"I knew I had to protect you." She finished, tears brimming her eyes. I nod my head, unable to speak much. We sit in silence for a while.

It's been four hours since I got to her bedside and the ambulance that's going to bring her to the psychiatric hospital is here now. She moves over onto their stretcher and they apply the seatbelts. The nurse says since she is a flight risk and suicidal that she must be transported by ambulance to ensure her safety.

I look at her, "I love you, Bev."

"I love you, Brooke." She replies somberly, "I'll see you in a few weeks." And with that, she is wheeled out of the room and I am left alone with my thoughts.

I pull out my phone and scroll through pointless apps. My stomach begins to rumble and I walk to the kitchen. It has been a week and a half since Beverly checked herself into the psychiatric hospital. I haven't heard from her directly, but the staff at the hospital informed me it would be a few more weeks before she was home. Something about her not feeling ready. That's okay with me, as long as she is listening to and helping herself.

My phone rings as I cook myself some eggs. Reading the caller ID I can't tell if I am excited for this phone call or stressed about explaining myself.

"Hey! I'm glad you answered, I was getting worried." The voice says as I pick up the phone. I recall the millions of texts and calls I've received over the last one and a half weeks of major tunnel isolation.

"Hey sorry, I've been processing." If you call drinking alone *processing*.

"That's okay, are you feeling up for a beach day with everyone?" Janet asks over the phone, cautious but welcoming.

"Yeah, I think so." I say back after a few moments of thought, smiling to myself when I finally answer her.

"Awesome, be ready in 15!" She hangs up before I can respond.

I scarf down my eggs and finish the last drink of my coffee, heading to my room to get dressed. I pull out my dark green bikini with the black ties holding it tight to my body and my purple, thin, beach dress that stops above my knees. I step into my bathroom and run my hands through my beach-wave hair, curl my lashes, and comb out my eyebrows. One pair of socks and one pair of black converse later, and I am out the door with my bag.

I see Kasey's car parked in my driveway.

"Hey there, gorgeous." Kasey says as I approach his car, holding the door open for me.

"I'm so sorry." I blurt out, hoping he will forgive me for the extended radio silence. Crashing myself into his arms, staying there for a few minutes, and letting go to sit in his passenger seat.

"Don't stress about it, babe. I'm here." He closes the door and smiles at me through the windshield as he walks around to his side and slides in, buckles up, and starts reversing out to the street.

Chapter Twenty Four

As Kasey parks his car in the lot, I see my friends already on the beach, laying out their towels in the most perfect spot. About 30 yards from the parking lot, mid-way between lot and water, with a large chunk of space between them and the rest of the beach-goers.

I have definitely missed the group beach days. Coming out at 11 o'clock in the morning with lunches and brews packed, staying until long after the sun went down.

Only leaving for more food but returning quickly to our spot. Nowadays, we leave a little earlier in the evening to visit our favorite bartenders and eat our favorite bar food for dinner. With the occasional return to the water after our night of drinking. *With a DD of course.*

It's a gorgeous late summer day, with a warm breeze making sand dance across the pavement around the cars. Blue skies with seldom clouds and easy surf. I take my shoes off after the first step into the sand, always a highlight. The sand feels comfortable as my feet slightly sink into it with each step, grabbing hold like a glove. My calves burn as I walk through it, always a workout.

Just a few feet away from my guardian angels now, they spot me and shriek of excitement. I totally pulled a Lily, being MIA and all.

"There she is!" Max shouts and jumps off his towel to hug me like it's been years.

"We missed you!" Janet yells, taking me in her arms while Lily does the same.

Korey looks at me from his towel, gives me a look, asking if I am okay and would approve of a hug, I shrug back. He stands and embraces me with his reassuring arms. "It's good to see you in the wilderness." He jokes, only I know it's not a joke. I haven't left the house much lately. Too busy "coping" and whatnot.

We all say Korey is the dad of the group, always protecting everyone as best he can. So I can only imagine how he's been feeling since I fell into the isolating sack of depression.

After the greetings, Kasey puts his hand in the small of my back and guides me to a spot next to Janet and lays out my towel for me to sit.

Enjoying the sunshine together, we pass Max's flask around. The ocean air smells refreshing and the light rays kiss my skin tenderly, reminding me why I love living here. The boys go for a long trip to the water while Janet, Lily, and I finish off the flask and talk. Finishing Korey's flask too as the boys return, drenched in saltwater.

"I'm starving!" Korey exclaims a few hours into our beach day, "I didn't bring food." He frowns like this is the worst thing in the world, dramatically throwing the back of his hand up to his forehead and letting out an exaggerated sigh, pulling giggles from everyone in the process.

"Well, dear, what does your stomach request?" Max says in a jokingly condescending way.

"BLAZER'S!" Everyone instantaneously agrees on the destination of our next adventure of the day. It is always an easy decision, we love to see Tilly and she loves to make our drinks strong for the same price as the "tourists" pay. (That's what we call non-regulars).

Max, Janet, Lily, Korey, Ashton, Kasey, and I all stand up, shake off our towels, and begin the hardest decision making of the day, who's driving who.

"How about we all meet at my house and then figure out the carpool situation from there?" I offer, hesitant to invite people into my home but simultaneously knowing they hold no judgment for me or my past *or present* issues.

Everyone files into their respective vehicles. Janet and Max in one car. Lily, Korey, and Ashton in another.

Kasey and I climb into his car and begin the quick drive to my house. When we arrive, I unlock the front door as everyone else parks either in my driveway or on the street.

The moment Lily gets inside my house, I pull her to the kitchen. "So, you and Ashton, huh?" I smirk at her and nudge her with my shoulder.

"We've been getting closer... A lot closer..." She winks at me, "Maybe don't disappear for more than a week and you'll get all the tea." She blows me a kiss and walks back to the living room with Ashton, Max, Janet, Korey, and Kasey.

I walk to my room to grab shorts and a T-shirt instead of my dress and as I cross the threshold, Kasey whispers after me on my heels.

"Brooke?" His voice sounds forcefully relaxed, trying not to come off as anxious.

"Yeah, Kasey?" I say as I open my dresser drawer and fish out a pair of light washed denim jeans.

"How are you doing?" He asks, not expecting much in return.

"Right now? I am *actually* okay." I smile at him, because it's true. I'm with my people and nothing could be better than that. "But I'll be real, I've been in a dark pit. Maybe I'll explain later?"

He lets out a breath of relief, "I'm so happy to hear that, and yeah for sure, but only if you're feeling up for it. Now let's go get food." Winking at me as he turns to leave and lets me change.

To go with the shorts I grab a random shirt from my closet and wind up with a black, cropped T-shirt with a faded

164

Nirvana cover album on it. Paired with my black converse and I am ready to go.

"Okay so I will ride with Max, Ashton, and Lily, why don't Korey, Kasey, and you drive together?" Janet says to me as everyone stands.

"Works for me." I reply, grabbing my purse and heading out the door last, locking it before climbing into Kasey's car.

When we get to Blazer's, Tilly's eyes light up the moment they meet mine. She runs around the bar and joins my group, "Babe! Where have you been?" She questions, hugging me so tight I can't breath.

"Oh you know, around." I wink at her and she goes back behind the bar. Grabbing a glass she looks at me, "Honey trap for you?" She says with excitement.

"Please!" I reply as she takes everyone else's orders. Kasey winds his arm around my shoulder, pulls my head to his and kisses my temple. It sends a shock of electricity through my body. We grab our drinks and head to our corner table on the patio, slipping right back into normalcy.

"I just don't think they need to know how much toilet paper I use!" Korey complains, not a care in the world as to who is overhearing.

"I mean I agree with you but why the fuck are they paying attention to that kinda shit? How much *are* you using?" Max says.

"Clearly enough to create a cause for concern." Ashton explains, "I don't know what you're doing in there but obviously your parents are tired of your ass."

We all roar with laughter from the pun Ashton unintentionally spit out.

Every one of us is now four or five drinks in, except for Kasey and I. Only on different ends of the spectrum. Kasey has had three drinks and two waters and I am easily seven drinks in, at least. My skin is feeling warm, my cheeks feel flushed, and there is a touch of nausea if I turn my head too fast. Kasey can obviously see my discomfort and stands without warning, walks inside, and returns a minute later with a glass of ice water. The way he cares for me in subtle ways makes my heart skip beats each time. And I'm not sure what to do with this feeling.

"Drink some water, please." He pleads, handing me the glass, condensation already beginning to trickle down the sides.

"Yes, sir." I respond, shakily grabbing the water and drinking half of it in once big gulp.

He kisses my temples and whispers, "Good girl." And my mouth is dry again. My head is spinning from feelings. The shock factor begins to sober me up a touch. Just enough to have coherent thoughts. I want nothing more than to get out of here and in his bed.

I back away, resting against the chair, looking at him with lustful eye contact. A smile takes across my face and I turn to Lily to change the topic swimming through my brain.

I'm sure it would be easy to pin my avoidant attachment style on the actions of Don Baring during my childhood, but that almost feels like a copout. Like too simple of an answer. Don't get me wrong, I fully believe his choices have forever altered mine. But I don't want that to be the truth. I don't want to be *that* fucked up from it that it forever affects my ability to show love, be loved, or my craving for affection, more than just in the bedroom.

But here we are.

Chapter Twenty Five

Eight years prior

I still have a hard time thinking I am safe at home. I constantly worried that he is going to break out of prison and come back here. Hurting me even more just out of anger. Or that he will tell someone else that he knows to come and hurt me out of spite.

Living in fear is odd to most people I assume. But to me, it's normal. Something I have become accustomed to, not that that's a good thing or should be romanticized. But living with a predator for 15 years really altered the chemicals in my brain.

Today is my 17th birthday. Two years exactly since Don was locked up and for once I don't open my bedroom door cautiously in the morning, afraid he will be waiting for me in the bathroom. Seventeen years I have been walking this earth. Seventeen years I have been trying to figure out what to do with my life.

I think it is finally starting to come together. I want to help other innocent children that were in my position. It's going to take a lot more therapy under my belt to get me to a point where I can take on other peoples' tragedies. But I think I can do it.

I walk into the kitchen and see my aunt sitting at the dining room table. Paper sprawled out in front of her. It's been 640 days since Beverly got out of rehab for her alcohol abuse. But 700 days since I saw her walk into the building.

"What's all that?" I ask, tapping her head on the way to the fridge to grab an Uncrustable, the strawberry flavor of course.

"Mortgage paperwork. Loan information. Bank statements." She pauses, setting down the tax information she's holding and rubbing her eyes. "I'm gonna sell the house."

I stop in my tracks. Realizing that this meant I will have freedom from the walls that watched every moment of exploitation I faced throughout my childhood.

"Is that so?" I reply, joining her while I unwrap my breakfast of champions.

"Yeah I figured it was time. I'm sorry I couldn't do it sooner." She looks at me with regret in her eyes, "I have a higher paying job now and think we can go somewhere a little nicer in the area."

"Well shit, that's fine with me!" My voice is muffled with food. I want nothing more than to leave this house. I haven't called it a home in years.

"Language." She says sternly even though I am nearly an adult now. "Have you looked into any colleges yet?"

The idea of college was both exciting and frightening for me. Leaving my aunt made me nervous because I know that most relapses happen in the first year, give or take. But excited because that meant I could get a taste of freedom.

"I applied to a few the other day but I haven't heard anything back yet. I still have hope though." Walking towards the trash can now I toss my wrapper in and my phone rings. "Love you Bev, it's Janet." And I walk to my room.

When I get to the beach I see my friends standing around the pier waiting for me. I run up to them and they shout with excitement.

"Heyo!" Max sings, hugging me and before passing me off to Janet. Lily smacks my butt and Korey twirls me by the hand.

"What's up guys?" I laugh at their goofiness, thankful to have them in my life.

"Oh nothing, just waiting on you as always." Korey winks.

"It's not my fault I live the furthest away!" I tease, "But hey, guess who's moving soon. Woop woop!" The looks I get in return are nothing shy of terrified.

"*Relax!*" Gosh, dramatic bitches. "I'm not moving *away*, just out of the house. Bev wants to go somewhere nicer."

"Well hell yeah! That's exciting!" Korey shouts, picking me up and spinning me around.

"Let's go!" Lily and Janet drag out the 'go' enthusiastically while Max fist bumps the air and jumps for joy, excited to be on the beach.

My friends have always had my back. Years ago, before Don got put away, Janet and I sat down and told them the honest truths about what had been going on. I wasn't forced to do it, I wanted to. So that I could have more love and support, since at the time I wasn't getting enough. And they delivered in more ways than I could ever ask for.

"I think we need to start bringing more food." Ashton whines while we are all sprawled out on towels taking up a good length of the beach.

"I think *you* need to start bringing more food." Max laughs, "You growing boy, you."

"Oh whatever, at least I'm not out of water." He throws back at Max, handing him the water anyway.

I stand up, stretching my legs and back before turning to the girls, "Y'all wanna swim?" They jump up and half follow, half chase me to the water. Laughing and yelling with me the whole way there.

The water here is perfect. And I don't say that lightly. It is a clean shade of blue with the kind of sand that sticks to everything because it's so fine and soft. The sky during the summer usually has no clouds whatsoever, which is fine because we use the ocean as our relief from the heat.

I honestly don't know what I would do if I didn't live near an ocean. It's vital for me. A release. A way for me to feel weightless and normal and sane. When I first jump into the water, all the stress of my current situation leaves my body as quickly as it entered. Even if only temporary, it was still helpful. Having my closest friends surrounding me during that only made it that much more healing.

A big issue in my mind lately is what I'm going to do when I leave for college. I know I still have some time left before that happens, but it weighs on my psyche regardless. I know Janet wants to go into a similar field as me, if I still want to pursue criminal justice. Neither of us know where we will get accepted. Max is most likely going to follow Janet, even if he hasn't admitted it yet, he loves her. Lily is planning on taking some time off before even *thinking* about going back to school, I know academics can be a struggle for her. And Korey, he has his life set out for him, working for his Mom's company. A little mom and pop mechanic shop near the edge of town. He is the one that is going to fix our cars when we get them, for the low price of a 6-pack of beer and parts.

"I should get home, my mom wants me to help her cook dinner for my Dad's birthday." Lily says disappointingly.

"Yeah I might as well head home too." I reply, standing to shake off my towel. Everyone does the same and we say our goodbyes, walking in our own directions to our own homes, except for Korey walking the same way with me for a little bit so our conversation doesn't die quite yet.

"How's your aunt doing?" He asks while grabbing my beach bag from me.

"She's doing okay from what I see. No relapses in sight and no random guys as coping skills. Very considerate." I say back, laughter added to the last part of my sentence.

"Well I guess that's good!" He chuckles back. "My parents decided not to divorce I guess. They're working things out. You know, therapy once a week, that kind of thing."

"I was just going to ask! That's good to hear. As long as it's good in your book too?" I hesitate.

"Yeah... I think it is." Korey smiles, a big beautiful grin with perfectly straight and pearly whites takes over his face.

"Good, I'm glad." I return the toothy smile.

Chapter Twenty Six

I groan slightly as I wake up this morning. My head is beginning to feel sore and my body is feeling the same. The light creeping around the curtains that aren't fully closed is the bane of my existence. Although, my hangover doesn't feel as bad as I'm used to.

I open my eyes, only to see I'm not in my room. I see a gray comforter wrapped around my body and a blue wall I've only seen one time before. I'm at Kasey's. I roll towards him and see him sleeping peacefully next to me. Not close enough to touch but still close enough to feel his warmth.

His eyes are closed and his forehead is soft, no wrinkles to be seen. With his mouth slightly open and his head rested gently on his pillow. I didn't think it was possible for him to look even better. He looks like an angel when he sleeps.

I look under the covers to see I'm wearing my own shirt and a pair of his shorts. Confused on how I got here and got in these clothes, I grab my phone from the side table next to me.

"luv u girl" From Janet.

"I know you won't remember, Kasey brought you to his place because you didn't want to be at yours alone. He was sober by the time we left. I like this guy for you" with a winking face emoji from Korey.

I love that Korey sends me little messages to help my morning confusion. I text him back to say my thanks.

"see u later" Janet had sent with too many "r"s.

Well, at least I know how and why I got here. But now my mind is running through what I said or did last night. Was I crazy? Did we fuck? Was I annoying? Was I embarrassing? Is Kasey going to hate me when he wakes up and sees I'm still here?

I slowly pull the comforter off of my body, getting off the bed slowly in an attempt to not wake the sleeping man I woke up next to. I creep into the bathroom and silently close the door. Rinsing off my face and using the toilet, I see the state of his bathroom. It's actually not too bad for a guy. Clean counters, some toothpaste splatter on the mirror (I am guilty of this too), a small pile of clothes next to the shower presumably from before we went out last night, with one normal towel and one beach towel hung up on the rack.

Returning to the bed, I try to get back in as subtly as possible. Kasey moans and stretches out his arms, finally opening his eyes.

"Good morning, sunshine." He says with sleep lacing his voice. Morning voice from Kasey is *sexy*.

"Good morning," I turn to him, "Uhm... Did we...?" My cheeks feel hot as I begin to ask.

He chuckles, "You think I would even try if you were so drunk you wouldn't remember getting here?"

I sigh, relieved. I'm hesitant to trust him because of my background, but the fact that Korey texted me good things and I woke up with my underwear still on, I'd say trusting him is the right thing to do.

"I'm sorry, I should've just gone home." I shy away self consciously.

"Don't apologize, babe. I like waking up next to you." He pulls me close, I can feel his heart beating in his chest. I like this.

"Did I do anything horrible last night?" I ask timidly.

He caresses my face with his warm, sleep laced hand. "Not at all." His raspy voice responds.

The eye contact alone is going to drive me mad. But in a good way. His eyes are so calming to look into. They lock my attention.

"Okay good," kissing his cheek as I say it. "Kasey?"

"Yes, Brooke?" His arm around my back now, tracing my spine with his fingers. Sounding mumbled and drowsy.

"What's your biggest goal?" Hurting to know more about him inside, I'm prepared for a comfortable morning with lots of talking. As much as we can.

He takes a few moments to think before describing his ideal future. "I want kids. And a wife to love. And I'd like to stay home with the kids a bit if my wife is okay with working, but either way is fine with me." Breathing in and out he continues, "A big house but I'm not picky on location and long as there is a good sized yard for a dog. As cliche as it is, I want a happily ever after."

I'm not sure what's turning me on more, his wanting kids, a dog, a big house, or a big family. But I like everything I'm hearing. And I can only dream that he would want that with me.

"I like that you've thought it out. I still feel stuck." My back grows goosebumps as his hand leaves the area he was touching.

"How so?" He rolls to his back and motions for me to rest my head on his chest. Continuing to trace my back with his fingers, I try to keep my train of thought moving forward.

"Well, I've always been scared of having kids. I'm scared I won't find the right person that would treat them, and me, correctly. My uncle kind of messed up that part of me." This will probably be the time I spill all my honest truths. But really, there's no better time. Laying in his bed, cuddling more than we ever have, a nice calming morning. "I know I want my career to be doing well before too many significant things happen in my life. I think it would just be easier that way."

He nods in agreement. Waiting for me to continue. "My uncle did some bad things to me. Actually, some horrible things. And I'm worried I won't be able to fully get rid of those memories and it will affect my kids."

After a moment of silence, Kasey speaks. "Well, I think you've been putting in a lot of work to rid your brain of those memories. But I also think those memories won't ever fully go away. And that's okay. That's how things work. You need to have *some* memory of them to help you protect yourself." He looks down at me, "I think your kids will be brilliant, beautiful, and not at all fucked up. Because you know what to look out for." I reach my head up and kiss his cheek once again.

His hand stops playing on my back and cups my face, pulling my lips to his. When they touch it's like a fire is lit in my stomach. Our lips move together for a long while before we break away for air, only to continue.

My body takes over before I can think and suddenly I am sitting on top of him, straddling his body with my legs. One of his arms wraps around me, holding me close as my hands begin to explore his shirtless body. His breath hitches as my hand moves farther down his stomach, pausing before anything risky happens.

I pull away and he's smiling at me. The biggest smile I've ever seen across his face, "Why'd you stop?" He asks me desperately and breathlessly.

"I need breakfast," I slid off of him to my respective side of the bed, "And as much of a meal you are, you don't count." I wink at him. He groans and sits up, reaching for his glass of water on the little table next to his bed.

"Thank you for opening up to me a little." Kasey says as he stirs our eggs in the pan on his stove. The rest of his house is nice, there's lots of good decor and his roommates seem nice.

"Thank you for the eggs." I say back, smiling at him from the small dining room table.

He sets down my plate in front of me, complete with eggs, toast, and strawberries. As well as a mug of freshly brewed coffee. Taking a seat across from me, he speaks between bites of breakfast,

"I'm sure it wouldn't compare, but I didn't have the easiest time growing up either. My parents weren't great when I was little and my mom constantly had her door locked and wasn't around. My dad worked too much to notice. At first I was too little to understand why my mom was sleeping all the time and had so many friends and why there were always spoons left in the bathroom. Once I got to the 8th grade, that's when we had sex ed and health class where they taught us about drug and alcohol abuse and I started to put all the puzzle pieces together."

I'm shocked. I had no idea he had such a difficult upbringing. He hides it well, that's for sure. But I guess most of us that can relate will try to hide it. I process his words before speaking. "First of all, it's not a competition. Second of all, that sounds horrible, I'm so sorry you had to go through that." I truly did not expect that.

"It's alright, it's part of what makes me, me. It doesn't define who I am but it helped shape me." He says calmly, at terms with his history.

"Well, I think you turned out pretty great, Kasey." I smile at him, "No doubt about that."

He blushes back at me, "So did you, Brooke." And we finish eating our breakfast with light conversation now, not so much prying into history.

Once finished, he grabs my dishes and puts them in the dishwasher with his, and guides me back upstairs.

"I'll get you home, do you want to hang out today? Or should I let you be?" He asks as we walk into his room.

"Maybe just my house for a change of clothes?" I ask, he smiles in return.

"I can do that." He replies, with a content voice.

"I'll message the group and see what everyone is up to, I also need to update them on my aunt. You okay with being there for that?" I say while grabbing the pants I originally wore here.

"If you're okay with me being there." He says changing his shirt in the bathroom. I can see a sliver of his skin littered with tattoos, but it's not enough. I want more.

Chapter Twenty Seven

Janet and Max are the last to arrive at lunch. Lily got here right after Kasey and I did, and Korey was already waiting at the table with water, chips, and salsa for everyone. Kasey and I sit next to each other with Korey on my other side, and Lily, Max, and Janet sit across the table.

"I'm starving!" Janet exclaims once we are all seated, "I need some serious grub."

"Mexican food was definitely the way to go." Korey says, looking at me.

"Yeah I was here with Bev a while back and it was good." I say to everyone. I'm nervous about this lunch date. I'm going to be telling them about Beverly and what's been going on. Basically I'll be explaining why I was MIA and the trouble Bev got herself into.

I'm pretty mixed on the whole "suicide is selfish" thought process people have. I can understand that view point, but I also have been in a position, on several occasions where I want nothing more than to stop breathing. To give up. To put all my traumas to rest, finally. I have wanted to pick up the bottles and not put them down until my muscles give out and drop them to the floor. I have wanted to let the voices and the thoughts win once and for all. "Suicide is the easy way out" they say. No, *dumbass*, it's the relief from unthinkable things that have happened to you. It's the escape from the things that keep us up at night. The escape from things that we never asked for but were given. The unspeakable. I am not responsible for *other peoples'* reactions to *my* choices. And that's that.

After putting in our orders with the waitress, Janet asks me, "So, Brooke. What's been going on?" She takes a sip of water. "We have all been wanting to bug you but we know you have to solo cope sometimes."

"Yeah so, about that. I'm sorry for disappearing like that. I just didn't really know how to handle this." I wave down the waitress. "So that night I went to your place," I say looking at Janet, "Don had hurt Bev just like he used to do to me. And she had gone to the hospital, that's all fine. She got home a few hours later I guess." The waitress comes over and I order myself a margarita, needing some liquid courage.

"Yeah, Janet told me about you staying that night, before you were MIA." Lily says and Max looks at me with kind eyes.

"So more happened that night." I pause.

"Did that motherfucker come back?" Max's voice is laced with anger, ready to find Don himself. His hand on the table now clenched in a tight fist.

"No, nothing like that." I take a drink from my fresh margarita. "But something happened with Bev." I don't know how they are going to take this news. Especially Janet, she has gotten close with Bev over the last few years, since she's been sober. And Korey has always loved talking with her after our beach days when we stop by before the bar. Lily has never gotten *super* close with her. But sober Beverly is hard to not love. She's the 'mom' you can go to with things that bother you and get some sound advice.

I am so thankful for the improved relationship Bev and I have had since she stopped drinking. But I can't help but wonder, if we hadn't fixed the connection, would I have needed MIA time to cope? Would it have bothered me as much to hear she attempted suicide?

The group is silent. They are trying to process the news I just shared with them. "But on the plus side, I think she'll be home in the next week or two. I'm sure she'd love a visit from each of you once she's settled in." I say, breaking the soundless table, trying to warm people back up into conversing.

"Fuck, Brookey. I'm so sorry." Lily empathizes.

"I'm glad you're here and doing relatively alright, you know we love you always." Max looks at me as he speaks, to make sure I really hear his words.

Korey gives me a side hug, "I'm sorry, girl."

"Why didn't you call me?" Janet is worried, I can hear it in her voice. "I would have isolated *with* you." She gives a light chuckle to lighten the mood despite a tear on the rim of each eye.

"Brooke, I'm shocked. I don't even know what to say." Kasey is the last to speak. He doesn't know what I meant by Don hurting Bev like he used to hurt me, but I'm sure his imagination is running rampant. He moves his hand to my thigh and gently begins to run his thumb across my leg. His touch calmed the leg that has been mindlessly bouncing up and down uncontrollably since I sat down at this table.

"I'm alright. I went down the hole. But I stayed alive, I took care of myself, I kept breathing. I'm here." I say to everyone at once, taking turns looking at each of my people. "Now, let's move on. You know she won't want to be babied, and neither do I."

"I can work with that. But, only if you promise to reach out if you need to. Even if you don't think you need to. We are here for you and we want to support you." Korey says to me.

"Deal." I smile back. We continue eating until our stomachs are full and our minds are happy.

"So what's next?" Max questions as we step out of the refreshing AC of the restaurant and into the hot atmosphere of the pier, a light saltwater breeze dances through our hair.

"Evening beach slash bar time? Only this time we bring the bar to the beach. We all need a little water therapy, liquor included." Korey suggests. "You should call Ashton, get him out there too!" He says to Lily.

"Okay!" Lily gets all giddy at the mention of his name and pulls out her phone, walking from the group to call her lover boy.

We head to our cars and all run home to grab our beach things. I assume Max is on Tequila duty, as it's his job.

I lay out my towel first and everyone follows suit. Being with a large group at the beach and all being in one solid line makes it difficult to share liquor. So we make up two rows, one of four, the other of three. I've got Kasey and Janet on either side of me, Max on Janet's other side. Korey, Ashton, and Lily are 'below' us.

As I suspected, Max brought a flask of Tequila. Only he surpassed my expectations and brought four. "I didn't know how long we'd be out here or how fucked up we wanna get. And we're all within walking distance of home and the cops already know our cars." He'd said when he pulled them out one by one and got surprised exclamations from the group for each one to come into sight.

"Works with me!" I say reaching for one and taking a swig followed by a drink of the bottle of OJ he brought with. I lay out on my towel, soaking up some sunshine. I can feel the ocean air lessening the harsh rays of sun beating down on my skin.

Kasey grabs the flask and takes a sip with no chaser, then bends over to me and plants a kiss on my temple. Making goosebumps appear on my legs. He brushes the strand of hair out of my face as I look at him, using my hand to protect my eyes from the light. "What was that for?" I ask.

"You just look really good." He says, not caring who else hears him. I blush, "Oh please." I say back.

"Look at those two cuties!" Janet exclaims excitedly.

"How adorable!" Max agrees with her. Lily smiles at us and kisses Ashton on the cheek.

Korey fakes a gag but then smiles and laughs."It's about time, honestly." And everyone harmonizes their agreement.

Kasey stands up, brushing the sand off his legs. "Hey boys, wanna go swim?" He asks Max, Ashton, and Korey and they all stand up with him, running to the freedom of the ocean. It makes my soul warm to see them spending time together.

Us girls immediately prepare for gossip time. I sit up and use my arms to hold myself, Lily flips onto her stomach, and Janet sits criss-cross.

"So, how's it going with Ashton?" I ask Lily, wanting juicy details.

"It's going so well. He understands bipolar disorder so that's been helpful, he cares about me, and he's super hot. Not to mention the sex is great." She takes a sip of Tequila,

"But we can catch up on that later, how are you doing with the Bev thing?" Her voice turns concerned.

"I'm fine, I promise. It was difficult to deal with at first, but I honestly can't blame her. I used to live through that shit all the time and I wanted so badly to get away from it." I drink from the flask, "It's gotten easier with time and the fact that she's alive is what matters. I'm truly okay." I say back to them, trying to convince them. But it was honest, it was truthful. Beverly had a moment and she's trying to get better. She'll be okay and that's the important fact.

"Okay fair, we believe you." Janet says.

"Now let's get back to Ashton?" I question, side-eyeing Lily with playfulness in my voice.

"Yes please." Janet seconds.

"He really is sweet. He loves to cook as well, and he's good at it." She winks.

"That's so good. I need to get better at cooking, too. I can do like one or two good dishes but otherwise it's ramen for days!" Janet laughs.

"I feel that!" I say to Janet, "What about you and Max? Everything good there?"

She takes a drink as well, "Yeah things have been great! We started cooking a semi-fancy dinner once a week to try and spend more quality time together and it's been so nice!" She explains.

Janet continues for another minute or two before the boys come back. Sopping wet they all stand over us and shake their heads like dogs, splashing us with water.

Chapter Twenty Eight

Janet screams, now sprinkled with droplets of saltwater. "I'm gonna get you back!" She yells as she stands and begins running after the boys.

Lily and I are relaxing alone now and she turns to me. "I'm glad you're alright. I really am, I don't know where I'd be without you." She takes a drink, "I love you, B."

"I love you, too." I say. "But you'd still be here and you'd still be fine."

She moves onto my towel and hugs me before returning to her spot and soaking up some more sunshine.

It's perfect today. Warm, but the water keeps the suffocating heat at bay. The ocean is a soft, light blue at the shore and a deep, calming blue farther out. The sky is holding onto every last bit of sunshine it can, keeping the clouds out of our view.

The group and I are starting to get tired of the beams. We've been out here for a few hours and the sunshine can drain you fast.

"I think it's time to continue this extravagant outing at Blazer's!" Max says, looking to the group for confirmation.

"Not after a cold shower, though." I say, standing up and dusting sand off my body. I struggle catching my balance when I first get up and Kasey reaches his arm out, not close enough to provide any actual support. The attempt is sweet.

"I second *that* shit." Lily agrees with me. Also stumbling as she gets up. Thankfully Max drove Janet, Ashton drove Lily and Korey, and Kasey drove me.

"Meet y'all there!" Janet says.

I climb into Kasey's front seat at the same time he does. He looks over at me and asks "You okay?" Turning his car on and switching into reverse.

"Just a little tipsy." I answer back, feeling bubbly inside. I look over to Kasey as he drives us to my house, the first of two pit stops on the way to Blazer's. "Can we just grab clothes at my house?" I ask him, hoping he catches on.

"You don't want to shower before we go?" His soft, puzzled eyes glancing away from the road to meet my lustful gaze for a brief moment.

"No I do." I study his profile. Strong features that aren't necessarily harsh. A kind of jawline that portrays confidence. A small amount of stubble, just enough to show he could grow a beard if we wanted one. His tattoo sneaks up from the collar of his shirt to behind his ear. One arm draped on the steering wheel while the other rests in his lap.

"I can wait for you if you want?" He offers.

"I was thinking I could shower at your place," I start. "To save some time, you know?" I finish my question. Not as timid as I would be if I were sober.

His breath catches slightly from shock. "Uh, yeah." Clearing his throat he continues, "That's fine with me."

He moves his free hand to my lap, resting on my upper thigh. Tracing the faded scars across my leg. We hadn't talked about those yet. But I know he's noticed them. I've seen his eyes trail my body enough times to know they weren't missed.

"I'll be fast!" I say, kissing his cheek and running into my house to grab a change of clothes after he parks in the driveway.

We pull up to his house, parking on the street because his roommate isn't home yet, "I don't want to get blocked in." He explains.

"I wouldn't either, that's why I love having a two car driveway with *only* two cars at the house." I laugh. Grabbing my backpack with clothes for me, he jogs to open my door. I grab his hand on the way out and as I turn to the front door, his arm slides into its newfound spot on my lower back.

I walk into his bedroom and go to sit on the edge of his bed when I am stopped. His hand grabs ahold of mine and spins me around. My body collides with his, our faces stopping inches apart. His blue eyes piercing my green ones, silently begging. I feel his heart trying to escape his chest, beating against mine. He walks backwards with me close to him, turning us and pressing me against his closed bedroom door.

"I can't help myself." His low voice says, trailing his hand up and down my back. Searching for more.

My breath shudders. He can read my body language and turns my face to the side, kissing down my neck sending flutters down my arms and legs. My feet barely feel planted on the ground.

He pulls away, a teasing look in his eyes. "Go shower." He demands softly, happy with his sexual taunt. I slouch away as his hands fall off my skin. He steps to the side allowing me to walk past, as I do, I slip off my shirt and drop it at his feet and walk into his bathroom. I close the door and turn on his shower. Letting my pants and bikini bottoms fall to the ground, there's a soft knock at the door as it opens. Kasey tries to hand me a towel, but I am already in the shower so I watch him set it on the counter and get frozen in place by the sight of me.

"Want to join me?" I ask, my voice sounding calm but my insides are the opposite.

"You sure, babe?" He asks, already tearing off his shirt.

"Yes." I answer firmly, unable to wait any longer.

He slides his shorts down his legs and opens the blurred glass shower door, stepping inside and moving under the water. His hair absorbs the water as the rest drips off his face and body. I can see his tattoos more clearly now.

There's a decorated snake trailing down his bicep, ending just below his elbow on the front of his forearm, next to that he has a clock, stopped at a specific time. There's words on his chest and I see the scattered roses, abstract designs, a mocking bird, and so much more painted across his body. His ink allows hardly any empty skin to see the sunlight.

"Brooke?" He says, tenderly.

"Yes?" I reply.

He says nothing back. His hand wraps around the back of my head while the other finds its way around my waist, pulling me close again. His lips crash into mine and my breath stumbles. I can feel the warm water from the shower raining down onto us, trickling between our bodies. The contrast of his warm skin and the cold tile against my back excited me. My hands wrap around his neck, holding him close. I don't want to lose this again.

Our lips are almost inseparable. I gently grab his hair, gripping it in my fingers. The hand he had glued to my back moves around the front of me. I can feel it slowly moving down my stomach, he pauses, parting our lips asking for permission. When I kiss him back he understands. His thumb trails across my clit softly causing my breath to quiver. I can feel myself warming, his groan of approval when his finger finds its way inside me tells me all I need to know. One finger at first, awaiting approval.

I moan into his mouth, lusting for more. He plays for a few minutes, causing my mind to spin. Not sure how to handle this, my hand pulls harder on his hair. He removes his fingers and looks at me, his eyes vibrant and full of feeling. I open my mouth and lick myself off his fingers.

He groans, "That. That was hot." Turning me around to face the crisp wall of the shower, I press my hot face against it. Yearning to be so close to him that we mesh into one being. Not knowing where he ends and I begin.

"I want more, baby." I say and he delivers.

"I want you. I've wanted you for so long." Kasey says as he bends me over slightly. Making it easier for us to be closer than we ever have. My mouth opens as I feel him brush up against me. I can feel him teasing me, wanting me to beg for it. I don't know if I can wait any longer.

Finally, I feel his cock thrust inside of me. Softly at first. Slowly increasing the speed and depth of each stroke. My body shudders from pleasure and my mouth gapes open. Kasey grasps my hair in his fist, using it as leverage to keep me where he wants me. I moan with every movement, he whispers into my ear, "Is that good, baby girl?"

It's difficult to hold enough oxygen in my lungs to respond.

"Yes." Was all I could manage to get out.

He starts going faster. Deeper. I have nothing to grip and my hand slides across the shower wall, desperately looking for something to help keep me in place.

My feet are tingling and my head is giddy. The water starts to feel colder as we begin to reach the best part. His moan sends me over the edge and I feel myself pulsate around him, yelling out in satisfaction. Not caring if his roommates are home yet. This must have done it for him because he quickly removes himself and releases his angst onto my back.

Heavy breathing from both of us as I turn around, smiling at him. One arm supporting himself against the wall while the other is wrapped around his length, gently stroking himself. He smiles at me, "It's about fucking time," he says as he presses his lips to mine once more.

"You're telling me," I say back, my legs shaking, "Now give me some of that water, a girl is cold." I giggle.

He chuckles back, "Yes ma'am." And he steps aside, turning the water temperature up just a touch. We finish the shower normally, washing the sun and sex off our bodies. Small talk makes the situation feel comforting.

"Do you know where you're going to work after nursing school?" I ask him while rinsing soap off my body.

"I'm not quite sure yet, but I have no restrictions either. Open to anything and anywhere." Kasey smiles at me when he speaks, making my cheeks turn a shade of pink.

"What?" I laugh awkwardly.

"I just want to be near you, if I can." He replies, kissing my forehead before climbing out of the shower and wrapping a towel around his waist.

Chapter Twenty Nine

Kasey and I are the last to arrive at Blazer's, which for everyone waiting on us, gave away what we were up to. I'm sure my pink cheeks didn't help at all. My sunflower yellow shirt is cropped just above my belly button ring and my jean shorts are light washed, of course rocking my black Converse. Kasey is wearing a deep green shirt and black jeans, which compliment him so well. We aren't necessarily matching, but the colors blend well together and it makes me smile when I realize it.

"Look who decided to show up!" Korey says, laughing and taking a drink from his beer.

"It's about time!" Janet shouts jokingly, I can see her eyes thirsty for the details. Lily smirks at me.

"I'm gonna get us some drinks," Kasey says to me, "And we weren't *that* far behind!" He play-shouts at the group as he goes to get us some alcohol.

I sit down next to Janet at our round table on the patio. They won't press the issue too much with the boys around, right?

"You know what's coming later, bitch." Janet nudges me, screeching quietly out of excitement.

"Oh stop it," I blush harder, "I know, I know."

Kasey returns with a Honey Trap and shot of Tequila for me and an Old Fashioned for himself. Sitting next to me, he drapes an arm around my shoulder.

"How's it going?" Kasey asks the group.

"Not too bad. I'm starving." Ashton says and everyone mumbles in agreement. We go to the bar in groups of two to order our food. Partly so no one takes our table, mostly so we don't overwhelm Tilly.

I feel safe when I am with my people. I could be going through one of the most difficult times in my life, but if I am surrounded by my closest friends, things feel alright. I worked hard to get where I am now, and I am so thankful that my friends stuck with me through all of it.

They have supported me, loved me, and treated me like a normal person. Despite my past. They make the trauma I endured a little more manageable. It hasn't been easy, don't get me wrong. On several occasions I had my friends "rescuing" me from myself. Spending the night with me to make sure I was safe, doing house calls, bringing me food to check in, and occasionally checking in with Beverly when I wasn't at my best or wouldn't answer my phone.

Janet, Lily, Max, and Korey have stuck with me. They have taught me more about what healthy love looks like, especially Janet and Max. They have been the relationship figure I've needed to see, to know what I should and shouldn't settle for. I am thankful for all of them. I love all of them.

"Hey baby, can you get me another drink?" Janet slurs, drunkenly asking Max for more liquid fun while clinging to his arm like she might slip into another universe.

"I can get you some water," Max says with a grin as he stands, kissing Janet's forehead.

"Fine." Janet pouts, yet she is ecstatic when the water is placed in front of her. "Ooh, yeah." She says as she drinks down most of the glass in one go.

Tilly brings our food to *our* outdoor patio table. It looks fucking delicious. Granted, it's bar food. But hey, don't shit on our bar, only we are allowed to do that. No one can wait to dig into their sloppy intoxication meal.

The best possible things you could eat while intoxicated at your local, friendly dive bar in which you frequent. Korey moans into his food, raising a belly laugh from everyone else sitting at the table.

"*What?* These are fucking *delicious!*" He exclaims, moaning again into the next bite of buffalo wings he takes.

"You are ridiculous." I laugh in his direction.

"How's everyone doing?" Korey asks, obviously feeling the alcohol running through his blood, apparent by the slur of his words.

"I'm doing better now!" Janet says as she kisses Max's cheek, whispering something only they can hear into his ear. Max's face changes into mush and he clears his throat.

"I think we are gonna, uh, head out." He stands abruptly and grabs Janet's hand on the way up and she laughs and smiles lustfully. "Get home safe everyone!"

"Are *you* gonna be safe?" I call out to Max.

He turns his head to yell back, "Always!" They walk inside Blazer's to pay their tab and head home.

Korey, Lily, Ashton, Kasey, and I are left at the table. All of us are feeling drunk but not hammered. A perfect level to continue if I do say so myself. Kasey speaks after a moment, "Anyone want to play darts?" He asks.

"Yes please!" Korey and Ashton announce in unison.

Lily and I look at each other and respond together, "That's all you guys." The boys stand up and go inside. Ashton and Kasey return a minute later with a drink for Lily and I while Korey reserves a dart board.

Once the boys are gone, Lily turns to me. "So, whatcha got?" She asks, beaming. I know she wants all the juicy details. And I know Janet wants them, too. I'll get to Janet later.

"Girl. He is incredible." I begin, "I felt the sexual tension like crazy but that was much better than I could ever even imagine." I go on to get her up to speed, answering all the questions she has.

"So you really like him?" She's smiling huge now.

"I really do, Lil." I take a drink of my Honey Trap. Unable to contain my excitement.

"I'm so glad, B. You deserve something good." She holds up her drink and I do the same. She continues to fill me in on what I've been missing while I was gone. Nothing too exciting but from what she says, Max and Janet are doing great which is great to hear, they are my example of good, healthy love.

I missed my friends. Spending all that time alone in my head made me realize how thankful I am to have my group. Being isolated is so comfortable sometimes, but being with them is comforting in a different way. I sat so low in my depression hole for so long, it feels like a second home when it creeps back. It's hard to pull myself out of it. I'm glad that Janet threw down the ladder for me.

I want to stay out of the hole if I can. I know I can. I did for so long, I just need to get myself back together. And I think today with my friends *and Kasey* was the perfect start in doing that.

Plus, Beverly should be home soon. And she might need extra help at first. Adjusting to her new life with whatever skills she learned while she was getting treatment. I need to be good for her, and me obviously. But also her.

Chapter Thirty

Korey, Ashton, and I are playing darts inside while the girls sit on the patio, I'm sure they are giving each other some secrets or juicy details. That's what girls do. I throw the first dart in my turn and get a great reaction from the boys. I hit a damn bullseye.

"There you go, dude!" Korey shouts.

"Atta boy!" Ashton adds, slapping my back.

"Thanks guys" I laugh, "That was totally a fluke!" I take a drink and hand the darts to Korey.

"So Kasey. You and Brooke, huh?" Korey says to me. I know they are close friends, but honestly I'm not feeling threatened by him at all, he just has that vibe.

I smile, my cheeks gaining color. "Yeah, me and Brooke."

"She's a sweet girl. Just know she's had a hard go at life and she doesn't need to take more shit from anyone." Korey says, firmness in his voice letting me know he means business.

"Yeah I get that, I didn't have the best time either growing up so I can understand it." I throw my dart as he replies.

"I think you're cool. And I think y'all are cute. I just have to look out for her. Ya know?" He tosses his dart and smacks the center of the board. "Woo!" he yells, high fiving Ashton and I. "We all want the best for her. I'm hoping that's you."

"Yeah man, of course." I say, respecting his words.

Ashton comes back with another round of drinks and the alcohol is starting to catch up to me.

"Last game?" Korey says, "We gotta check on the girls soon." His words were laced with liquor.

"Yeah, I'll go first!" Ashton announces as he picks up the darts from the tall table our drinks are sat on.

Ashton, Korey, and I walk through the door to the patio and the first thing my eyes land on is Brooke's grin. She's looking at Lily like she's listening to the most important story she's ever heard. The shirt she's wearing is teasing me, showing off her boobs in an innocent way. Knowing what the shirt is hiding makes me even more excited. Her hair is glistening in the evening sunshine and her eyes are lit up like they are the sun itself. If the sun was forest green. She looks over at me, tucking her hair behind her ear as she does so. Her eyes sparkle.

I sit down next to her, setting down two glasses of iced water that I'm sure we both desperately need. Lily says something I don't hear and Brooke bursts out in laughter, the happiest sound I have ever heard.

"Thank you, baby." She says as I kiss her cheek. Ashton sits down next to Lily, also delivering well needed water, and Korey sits between Ashton and I. I'm glad I was able to bond with them a little more over darts. It's important to me that Brooke's friends like me.

The conversation carries over many different topics, school, life after school, families, jokes, and some newfound drama involving people we don't associate with anymore.

"I'm not sure where I wanna go, I don't even know which field exactly I want to use my *genius* knowledge in." Brooke says.

"Well, whatever you decide, you'll be kickass at it." Korey responds to her and then turns to me, "What about you? Ideas on where you wanna be a nurse?" I hate this question because there are so many places to go and I can't decide.

"I've thought a little about it, but nothing sticks out."

Brooke stands up to go to the bathroom and her foot doesn't clear the leg of the chair, she trips sideways for a split second before I steady her with my hand around her waist. She giggles and tells Lily to join her. While they are gone, Korey gets another drink and it's just me and Ashton.

"Bro real talk for a second, Arlo? On the top of my shit list."

"What'd he do this time?" He asks.

"Keeps talking shitty about Brooke and saying if I don't get her soon he's gonna swoop in and use her up." I say back, taking a big drink of water. I need a clearer head.

"Fuck him. You know he won't do shit and just thinks he can because he never had consequences growing up. I'll kick his ass *with* you if it has to be done." He finishes his drink.

"Thanks man, it's just grinding my gears because I live with him. And I overthink bringing Brooke over."

"You're two floors above him with a lock on the door, no stress." Ashton says.

"Good point." I shrug and think about the locking doorknob I installed shortly after I moved in.

Korey gets back with a round of shots for everyone, borrowing one of the bartender's serving platters to carry them. He excitedly sets them down on the table and starts putting one in front of every seat at the table. Minus the two that Max and Janet left empty. The girls return a minute later, screeching at the sight of Tequila and limes sitting on the table.

"Oh fuck yeah!" Lily says eagerly. She picks up her glass and lime, waiting for someone to decide what we are toasting.

"Thank God." Brooke exclaims, "I was drying up!" She throws her head back in laughter. It's the most beautiful thing to witness. The way wrinkles form in the corner of her eyes, her cheeks reddening from joy, it's incredible to see.

Ashton, Korey, and I all pick up our glasses, holding them in the air and Korey shouts "For having a good fucking time! All the time!" And we all throw back our Tequila and suck on our limes. Brooke and I make eye contact while chewing our tangy chaser and begin to laugh at each other for the silly faces we are making.

Her eyebrows furrow at the sour lime and her cheeks get pink from the sudden Tequila in her body. She is gorgeous.

We keep drinking late into the night. When it's time to leave, we all pay our tabs and drunkenly walk out the front door.

"Everyone's walking, yesss?" Lily slurs.

"Yes sir!" We all say in unison with laughter. Lily and Ashton begin walking towards his house, Korey joins them for a while before parting ways, and Brooke and I walk to mine. Taking our shoes off when we get inside my room and slumping straight into bed. She pulls her pants off and moves close to me.

"How are you feeling, baby?" I ask, only to hear heavy sleep-fueled breaths in return. I pull her closer, kiss her cheek, and doze off.

Chapter Thirty One

My head is throbbing before I can even register where I am. When my eyes open and I see his soft features glowing in the morning light, I feel safe. Comfortable. I remember the beginning of last night, but not leaving Blazer's or getting to Kasey's. I roll away from him and look at the nightstand next to me. My phone is plugged in and there's a glass of water and a bottle of Ibuprofen. I slowly sit up, open the bottle, take two pills and swallow them with a drink of water. I continue to look around the room and see my pants laying on the ground next to the bed and the light in the bathroom peeking out through the crack in the doorway.

Kasey groans as he adjusts his head on the pillow, opening his eyes and seeing me sitting up, he takes a deep breath, "Good morning, baby." He says, my heart jitters inside.

"Good morning, handsome." I say back after a moment. He reaches his hand out to me, asking me to join him. I lift the blanket and slide in next to him. His arm wraps around my waist and pulls me close to him, my head resting against his chest.

"Did you sleep okay?" He mumbles into my hair, sleep lacing his voice, making my body grow warm.

"Yeah, I slept good. What about you?" I ask. He yawns and kisses my forehead before responding.

"I slept amazing." I say, my phone pings but I ignore it, wanting to keep this moment in my grasp for as long as I can. His warmth brings me happiness and solace. His grasp makes me feel protected and safe.

"Thank you for the water and Ibuprofen." I add after lifting my head to kiss his cheek.

"Of course, you seemed like you'd need it." He giggles. "And before you ask, you fell asleep before I had even gotten into bed." He adds. Comforting me knowing that I was confused waking up without pants on. It feels good to know that he was respectful and knew that I was not in a place to give consent.

"Thank you." I reply. I hope he can see that I am grateful for him. Despite all my issues, I know that I can trust him. I can sense it. It seems like he is tough on the outside, but I have been seeing the softer side of him more and more.

I watch him standing at the stove in his kitchen, stirring our breakfast eggs in the pan. His shirtless body showing off his tattoos and muscular arms. The way he looks at me from across the room makes my skin grow goosebumps. I can't help but imagine him walking over to me and pinning me against the wall, carrying me upstairs and throwing me against his bed, not giving a shit if the eggs burn.

"Orange juice or coffee?" His voice pulls me from my inappropriate thoughts.

"Orange juice, please." I say back, shying away and looking down at my phone in hopes he won't see my cheeks turning red.

"You okay?" He asks, a hint of flirtation in his voice. He can definitely see my cheeks.

"Yeah, I'm happy." I reply with a smile almost reaching both my ears.

Back in Kasey's room I finally check my phone.

"u make it back ok?" Korey had asked me sometime after 3:30 in the morning. Were we really out that late?

I shoot him a quick reply, "you betcha"

"checking checking" in the group chat from Janet with replies from everyone.

"**hola**" from Lily.

"**Yes hi I'm alive!**" Korey replied.

"**Breathing but dying**" Max is the last message in the group chat. I send my proof of life and lock my phone.

Kasey walks into his room from the bathroom, sitting down next to me on the bed. He lays back and reaches an arm out to me so I will join him in laying down.

"What would you like to do today?" He asks, tracing the lighting-inspired tattoo across my shoulder and arm.

"Anything." I respond, feeling cozy resting my head on his arm, my leg sprawled across his.

He moves his hand down my back and grabs my butt, softly at first. He uses his other hand to turn and lift my face towards his and plants a kiss on my lips. Our lips move in harmony and I climb on top of him, my legs straddling his sides. His hand finds its way back to my butt and squeezes it harder. I move my hips across him and a soft moan escapes his lips.

His free hand grabs the back of my head and pulls me closer to him. My breath trembles as I move back and forth across his body. Feeling him harden makes me crave more. He bites my lower lip and I moan, that sends him over the edge and he wraps an arm around my back and flips us together so he is over me now. He pauses and looks me in the eyes, "Brooke…"

"Yes, Kasey?" I reply with lust.

"I want to fuck you." He growls and rips off his shirt, throwing it across the room, his chest defined and his arms littered in pictures. I want to dive into the meanings with him.

"Then fuck me." I say, out of breath.

He sits us up and slides my shirt off, throwing it across the room with his. He leans back into me and kisses my lips, then my cheek, and trails down my neck. He pauses to take off his pants and kick them aside. When he makes it to my stomach he slowly pulls down my pants as he kisses lower and lower. Teasing me with his tongue and lips, all around the place I want them without actually making it there.

"Please…" I beg him.

He suddenly finds my clitoris with his tongue and I suck in a sharp breath, letting him know he's on the right track. He plays for a while before trailing back up my stomach and chest and neck. Before his lips meet mine, he slides a finger inside of me and I let out another breath.

"You're so wet, B" he says as he's inside.

"That's your fault." I giggle back before he removes his finger and replaces it with his cock. He moans as he enters me, making shivers go down my spine and goosebumps show on my arms and legs. He moves his hips making his length go deeper, faster with each motion. My hands reach out on the sheets and grab whatever they can, twisting the fabric in my fingers. He kisses me during the earth-shattering act. My mouth gapes open and my breathing gets heavier. He can sense that I am getting close to climaxing and he slows down, I whine softly.

"Just making sure this is what you want, baby." He says, knowing damn well this is *all* I want.

"Do I need to beg?" I say, breathless.

"Maybe." He winks at me as he quickly enters me again and I let out a satisfied yelp. He pleasures me so well.

He continues to fuck me and my head spins. He grabs my legs and puts them in the air and then onto his shoulders as he continues to blow my mind. He places his hand around my throat and looks to me for approval, I set my hand over his and help him squeeze lightly, giving permission. My body is heating up and my heart is beating crazily. My hands grip the sheets tighter and he grunts with satisfaction from watching me squirm in pleasure.

He keeps up the same pace and it sets me off. My body trembles and I turn my head to the side to cover my mouth with my arm as I let out a huge moan. Fireworks go off as I release my stress. I look back at him and when he sees my flushed face, he erupts himself. Pulling out of me, leaving behind loneliness, and finishing across my stomach with a groan. He lays next to me and kisses my forehead on the way.

Panting and out of breath, he reaches for the water on my side of the bed and takes a long drink. He hands me the water and I follow suit. I hand him the now empty glass and he sets it on the nightstand. He gets up and walks into his bathroom, returning with a towel to clean himself off of me.

"We can afford to lose these ones." He winks as he uses the towel to wipe me off.

"These ones?" I ask, chuckling with confusion.

"Yeah, these swimmers. I've got enough for when we really want 'em." He replies. I am shocked. I've had thoughts about a possible future with Kasey but I hadn't thought about it in depth.

He must see my shock because he speaks again, "Not to totally freak you out, but you'd make an amazing mom. And I want to witness that, one way or another." He throws the towel into the bathroom sink and returns, kissing my red cheeks.

"You think so?" I ask him.

"I know so, baby."

Chapter Thirty Two

I woke up in my own bed this morning. Immediately I walk to the window and open my 'drug' box, grabbing a fresh joint that Kasey rolled me the night before. I light it with my black lighter and slide the window open.

I'm not super hungover this morning, thank God. Waking up without a blaring headache and light sensitivity is such an amazing change of pace. Why don't I do this more often? The salty breeze fills my room as it takes out most of the weed smell with it. For good measure, I light a candle on the way to the shower.

Beverly comes home today. A week after I updated the friend group about her situation. I am excited to have her home. But I am equally nervous to have her home. From what I heard, her job kept her position available for her. They were very understanding and are giving her another few days to relax at home before returning to the grind.

I get a phone call around ten o'clock. Climbing out of my shower still soaking wet, I answer the phone.

"Hello?" I say to the unknown number,

"Hi, I'm looking for Brooke." The voice says back.

"This is her." I reply.

"Good morning, Brooke! This is Karly from Sunrise Behavioral Health Center! Beverly is just about ready to head home and I understand you'll be picking her up, is that right?"

My heart skips. "Yes, that's right! When can I come get her?" I ask impatiently.

"Whenever you are ready!" Karly says back.

"Perfect, I'll be there in about 45 minutes!"

"See you then." She says. I hang up the phone and climb back in the shower to quickly finish rinsing off.

"it's time! im heading to get her!" I type in the group chat as I slide on my Converse, adding celebratory emojis.

"headed out to get Bev!" I send to Kasey as I walk out the front door. My phone starts pinging over and over and I grab it from my back pocket once I sit in the drivers' seat of my car.

"Go get your girl!" Kasey was the most recent to reply, showing up on my phone first, I heart the message and open the group chat.

"WOOP WOOP!!!!!" from Max.

"good luck B!" Lily had sent.

"Fuck yeah! Let us know if you need anything" Korey said.

"send her my love!" Janet said with a few heart emojis.

I drive 30 minutes to the inpatient center Beverly has been at for the last few weeks. When I park, I see her sitting in the lobby wearing gray sweatpants and a pink sweatshirt. Her hair pulled back in a simple, neat bun. I walk in the door and she jumps up, running to me and holding me tight.

"I missed you!" She says, holding back tears. Her voice makes me choke on my breath, I didn't realize how much I had truly missed her.

"I missed you, Bev. I'm so excited to bring you home." I say back, honest. "Let's go. You hungry?" I ask as we walk out towards my car, setting her bag in the backseat.

We walk inside the house and she takes a moment in the doorway. Looking around and appreciating what she gets to come home to. She sets her bag on the couch and sits down next to it. I join her and lay a pillow on her lap, laying my head on top of it.

"How was it?" I ask her, not wanting to tiptoe and make things awkward.

"It was actually really nice, I learned a lot about myself and I feel really good. Much better than rehab." She laughs. "Don't beat around the bush, okay?" She strokes my hair with her hand, "I'm good, I promise. And I will tell you if I'm not." She finishes by kissing her hand and pressing it to my head.

"Okay, fair." I say to her, "Just know I'm here for you."

"I know. Now! Tell me what I've missed in your world." She says excitedly.

"Oh, Bev. What haven't you missed." I joke with her. "The friends miss you, I'm a little more… Serious… With the person I was seeing before you left. Summer is almost over and I have to go back in three weeks so I am not excited about that. But overall, things have been good."

"I don't even know his name yet and you're getting *serious*?" She laughs, pressing me with her eyes for more details.

"His name is Kasey, and you'll love him." I say.

"Can I meet him?" She asks dramatically.

"Of course you can." I reply.

"Okay good, I'm gonna get some sleep in my own bed, I love you." She kisses my forehead and walks to her room for the evening.

This morning is another start to a smothering hot day, the birds outside my window are going crazy as they try to wake up the neighborhood.

Kasey replied very shortly after I asked if he was available to meet Beverly.

"I'd love to. When should I come over?"

I text back instantly, "right now, she's dying to meet you" with a wink face emoji. I walk into the living room where Beverly is watering her plants, "He's on his way." I tell her, "I'm gonna go change."

"Sounds good." She replies with a smile.

I walk into my bedroom and the smell of the weed from yesterday is lingering. I light another candle and place it on the windowsill with the still open window. My closet door smacks the wall as I slide it open and grab a blue T-shirt from a hanger. I pair it with a pair of black lounge shorts and slip on a pair of fuzzy socks that match the shirt. Knocking on the front door makes me jolt.

Suddenly I am extremely anxious. I have never brought someone home to meet Beverly. Not that I was seriously interested in, anyway. I've never introduced a significant other to my mother figure. What was she going to think? What was he going to think? What were we all going to talk about?

I open the front door and Kasey kisses my cheek as he walks in holding a bouquet of flowers, he walks up to Beverly and hands her the flowers, holding a hand out to shake hers and introduces himself. She swats his hand away playfully, grabs the flowers, and gives him a hug.

"Handshakes are too formal, don't be silly." She says. Beverly walks to the kitchen, placing the flowers in a vase with water and we all sit at the table. Kasey on my left and Beverly across from us. She looks, what she can see of him, up and down. Giving me an approving side eye. "So, tell me about yourself."

Kasey takes a breath and places his hand on my thigh, I can see his tension roll off his shoulders as he does so.

"Well, I am in the nursing program at college and hoping to graduate in a year but I'm not sure where to practice. I grew up around here and always saw Brooke in the hallways but it took us a while to actually be introduced." He gives her a moment to process. "Right now I live down the block with two roommates, both in college with me, one I love and one I hate." He laughs and so does Beverly.

"Those are all good things. Even the roommate thing because you can't love everyone. Not everyone is easy to love." She laughs back and looks at me.

"That's true, but some people are." He says back, gripping my thigh tighter and looking at me from the side.

Beverly and Kasey keep talking for a while, lots of laughing and joking around which is a very good sign. The three of us sit for almost two hours before my phone pings in my pocket.

"beach day?" Janet said in the group chat. Immediately Max, Korey, and Lily reply in agreement, causing my phone to erupt.

"That your people?" Beverly asks.

"Yeah. They want a beach day." I laugh.

"Well go! Have fun! Bring them all for dinner?" She says. "I need to grocery shop anyway and this is a good reason."

"You sure?" I hesitate to clarify because I don't want her to think I am beating around the bush like she asked me not to, but I'm surprised she's up for a dinner party so soon.

"Yes, I'm sure." She smiles.

Kasey and I pull into the parking lot at the beach and see everyone setting up their towels a few yards away. Before opening his door, he leans over to me and kisses me hard and deep.

"It was great meeting her." He says and looks me in the eyes.

"I think she loved you." I say back, smiling. "Nice job with the flowers, too"

"I had to at least try and impress. Yours are coming, don't worry." He opens his car door and walks around to mine, opening it for me and grabbing my towel and beach bag from the backseat.

Chapter Thirty Three

I leave to go back to school in two days. Two more days with Janet, Max, Lily, Ashton (who we've all grown close with), Korey, Beverly, and Kasey. All my people. The last few summer weeks with them have been so memorable. With missing memories of course.

I'm excited to be almost done with school, but I'm not excited to get back to it. Only a few more months of hell before I'm free to work for the rest of my life. Just one last semester.

I open my window and light up my joint, blowing the smoke out the window and feeling some of my anxieties go with it. I'm going to miss having my own space inside the house. Where I can rot in bed all day or get to the bathroom without needing to put pants on. Dorm life sucks. But I guess it's not all bad because you're not often lonely.

Beverly is doing really well, no other mishaps and she's been back to work for a few weeks and she's doing great there. It makes me feel better that I have to leave knowing she's better. She started seeing someone last week and while it's early, he seems kind and caring. They're cute together, too.

I rinse the lathered soap out of my hair and let the water run over my face. Warming my body and releasing my tension. High showers are *definitely* better than hangover-curing showers. I wrap the towel around my body and step out, lathering my arms and legs with lotion. My phone vibrates on the counter.

"You almost ready, baby?" Kasey texts, confirming he is picking me up for one last hoorah with our friends. The original group has adopted Kasey and Ashton, they are part of our crew. The boys love having guys nights and the girls love having sleepovers and shopping days.

"yeah just need 10 :)" I reply and set my phone down. I comb through my hair and put on mascara. Walking into my room, I put on my black bikini and a pair of black jean shorts with a forest green crop top. My beach bag sitting on the foot of my bed is ready to go and I fill my water as I walk through the kitchen. Beverly is sitting at the table eating avocado toast and drinking coffee.

"Beach day! Love you!" I yell to Bev as Kasey knocks on the front door.

I swing open the door and Kasey is standing there, as handsome as ever. Black T-shirt and blue swim trunks that make his eyes pop in my direction.

"See you later, Bev!" Kasey says with a wave in her direction.

"Have fun you two!" She responds and takes another bite of her toast. Happy that it's Friday and she's about to have a few days off.

I grab the bottle of Tequila from Kasey's backseat as we park in the lot, taking a large swig and shuddering at the taste. I hand him the bottle and he does the same, only with less of a reaction. He fills the flask with Tequila and hands it to me to put into my beach bag.

"Come on, B. Let's get out there." He says and gets out of the car. Before I can grab my bag and reach for the handle, he swings my door open. That's one of the many amazing things about Kasey, he opens my door as often as he can.

We are the first to arrive. I lay my towel out in the sand next to Kasey's and sit down. I hand him the bottle of sunscreen from my beach bag and he gladly takes it, putting sunscreen on my back and shoulders while I do my chest, arms, and face. The way his hands run over my skin is heavenly. Something I don't ever want to lose. Janet and Max walk up while I am lathering my legs.

"What's up, *beach*es!" She shouts an awful pun as they get closer. I laugh back at her.

Janet lays her towel down on my right and Max puts his down next to her. They start chattering as Ashton and Lily shout from the car, letting us know the party has arrived. At the same time Ashton steps in the sand, Korey comes from behind him and jumps on his back. I hear playful yelling and shouting while Kasey and Max run over to join them. Korey hands Lily his towel and the boys run out to the water. Lily sets her, Korey's, and Ashton's towels out in line with Janet, Kasey, and I's but closer to the water to create that square-like shape of people.

"Hey girl!" Janet says to Lily as she sits down on her towel.

"Hey loves." Lily says to both of us. She hands me her sunscreen and I start putting it on her back with no need for her to ask. We know the drill.

The boys come back dripping salt water. They sit on their towels laughing about whatever they were going on about.

"Hey pass the good stuff." Korey says, reaching a hand out for whoever will fill it with a flask first. Ashton, Janet, and I all throw our flask onto his towel and he shouts, "Damn! A three for one deal?" He laughs and takes a drink from mine, not knowing whose is whose. We always have *something* on us at the beach. How could you not?

My mind is racing, laying here in the sun soaking up as much as I can before it's back to life for a while. Thankfully I will be done with school in December. A little earlier than the rest of my class. Kasey is at the forefront of my mind, though. The way he treats me is unlike any way I've been treated before. The way he laughs with me is unlike any way I've laughed before. And don't forget the sex. The way he *fucks* me is unlike any way I've been fucked before. He is perfect.

His personality, his soul, his body, the way he does things, the way he says things, it's all perfect. We've had an argument or two but nothing that caused us to change our feelings. I'm scared to admit it, but I love him. I know I do. I don't want to go through my life without him being a part of it.

I want him.

"Y'all ready for one last Blazer's date?" Korey says to the group, a hint of sadness lacing his voice.

"Let's do it." I say to him, deciding for the group. We slowly stand and pack up our things. Shaking out our towels away from each other and putting our shirts on. We walk to our cars and when we get to the beginning of the lot, Max speaks.

"How about we stop at our place and we can walk there? For old time's sake, go back to our roots again." Everyone agrees, not only is it nostalgic, but we can drink a lot more if we aren't driving. And I have a feeling this will be our last big go around for the season.

Kasey and I pile into his car, Korey joining us since he walked here in the first place, and the other two couples in their cars. When we park on the street outside Max and Janet's. I start to get out but notice Kasey isn't taking his seatbelt off yet.

"You coming?" I ask, concerned.

"Yeah, I just want to talk to Korey for a minute. I'll be there soon." He says and kisses my cheek. I turn to look at Korey, he shrugs his shoulders.

I walk inside Max and Janet's and am met with an obligatory shot of Tequila. Korey and Kasey walk in a few minutes after I sit on the couch next to Lily and Janet, Kasey looking for me and smiling once our eyes meet. It makes me nervous thinking about what that talk was about. I'll try to ask later.

The late arrivals are handed shots and they throw them back with no complaints. Joining us girls in the living room where we all start talking.

"So, what the fuck are we gonna do without each other?" Janet says, I can see tears welling up in her eyes.

"What do you mean *without* each other? You're still gonna be annoyed as fuck with all my texts!" Lily responds, trying to make Janet laugh away the tears.

"Yeah... I'm gonna put the chat on do not disturb," Korey teases.

"Oh fuck off." Max says, "You could never, you'd miss us too much." He shoves Korey lightly.

"Yeah I know, I know." He admits, "I'll be lonely here."

"I'll still be here, so will Max." Janet says, waving her hands around the apartment they live in. They both do school online so they don't need to move anywhere right now.

"I'll be done in a few months and will come back for visits before winter break." I say, "Which is when I'll be *graduatin'* bitches!" I shout enthusiastically. Already thinking ahead for my freedom.

"That's right! You're getting out of there early!" Korey says, "See? We'll have all of us back together in no time!"

We sit and talk for a while. A number of shots and and two hours later, we are drunkenly putting on our shoes and heading out the door for Blazer's.

Chapter Thirty Four

During the walk, I look over at Janet, silently telling her that I need to talk to her. I need to tell someone about my fuckup and she is the least judgmental person I know. She nods back, saying that she will find a good moment to come to me. After we walk into Blazer's the boys order us our drinks and Lily, Janet, and I find a seat on the other side away from the games. There were too many people playing games for us to be able to talk together.

The boys return and the talks begin.

"I tried telling them I didn't want to work Sunday's, because most shops aren't even open Sunday's but they said they need me to take over our younger clients because my parents are too old and grouchy for them." Korey disappointedly continues the conversation the boys were having while ordering.

"Like I get it, old people don't work so they go during the week but still that sucks for your Saturday night adventures." Kasey counters.

"Let me know if you ever need a copout." Max replies, knowing he is close with Korey's parents and could most likely get him a Sunday off if he's in dire need.

Lily stands, "Can we go sit outside? It's getting stuffy in here with all these tourists."

Max groans in agreement and the rest of the group stands to follow. I look at Janet, pleading for a minute with her alone.

"I'm gonna run to the bathroom," Janet says to no one in particular and all of our friends at the same time.

"Yeah me too, be right out!" I piggyback off Janet as the group nods and walks out the door to grab our round table.

My anxiety skyrockets more with each step we take closing in on the bathroom. I don't know why I am so nervous. I am afraid she'll yell and scream at me or disown me as a friend or be so disgusted she tells the group and they all decide unanimously to hate me.

"What's up, babe?" She asks as the bathroom door closes and she bends over to glance under the stalls and check there's no feet dangling.

I freeze. I don't know how to start this conversation. I take a deep breath before I start, my hands instinctively twirls and plays with the rings I wear diligently.

"I did something bad." I finally say, her eyes harden and I can tell she's unsure where this talk is going. I continue before letting her mind spiral too far from earth, "I guess it could have been worse and no one is hurt or dead and everything is fine now."

"What happened, B?" She says cautiously.

"I got in an accident. In my car. I shouldn't have been driving but I was struggling with the Bev thing and all my memories of Don creeping back in and I fucked up." I say without taking a single breath. I watch as her face tightens then relaxes. She takes a breath before offering her support.

"Are you okay? I'm sure it was scary."

"I'm alright. My car is alright. No one else was involved so I just went home. I panicked."

"Understandably, but I'm glad you're okay. I can't not say the things so are you ready?" She asks, giving me a moment to prepare for the rightful best friend scolding.

"Go ahead." I say and look attentive, ready to take in her speech.

"What the *fuck* were you thinking? You could have killed yourself or someone else and I don't know what I would do if you were dead or in jail. There's plenty of other ways to get around when you're hammered that don't involve a giant beast of a vehicle that can literally kill. I love you *and* that was dumb. I love you *and* be smarter. I love you *and* don't be the next town tragedy. Don't do it again." She finishes by taking a breath. She rests her hand on my shoulder before pulling me close for a tight hug.

"I'm glad you're okay. Call me next time."

"I will, J. I love you." I reply, feeling her warm body hold mine for just long enough. She pulls away and says it back.

"I love you, B. But you have to tell Kasey. He won't be happy about it but he will be able to help take the burden off of you and be an ear for you to talk to. I will be too, but it's nice when there are multiple ears. The rest of the group would probably be more upset but you can talk to them too, if you want."

My head begins to spin and run through all the possibilities of telling Kasey and my friends. It seems like too much for me to handle. Too much for me to do. Too many people to see my weak spot. Janet can see the gears in my head on overdrive and the steam coming out the sides of my face.

"I'm not going to force you to tell anyone, it's completely up to you and what you're comfortable with." She says to me, recognizing the overwhelming look in my eyes.

"I'll think about it." I reply, wanting to wash down the lump building in my throat with a glass of something strong.

We join the rest of the group on the patio just a few minutes before Tilly walks out and sets down another round of drinks and some fries on the house. My mind feels more calm until Kasey finally catches my eyes in his, "You okay?" He quietly says to just me.

"Never better." I lie, planting my hand on his leg. I wonder if he can sense the sudden anxiety I feel from hiding something from him. To avoid those thoughts, I turn to the group, "Oh hey! I forgot to mention. Beverly said that dinner was a super good time and she loved seeing y'all. Don't ghost on her while I'm gone please. Check in with her."

Everyone nods their heads in agreement and we get back to spending our last day with our favorite people at our favorite place.

Tilly comes by to chat on her break, trying to hide her irritation from dealing with grumpy, old, drunk men. I can't imagine being a bartender and having to deal with creepy people that are too drunk to understand boundaries.

Chapter Thirty Five

I need to tell Kasey. It feels wrong to share my body with him without sharing my fuck up. I know that seems strange, but I have such a drive to be close to him and if that's not going to happen because of my idiotic, drunken mistake, I need to know sooner rather than later.

I'm sure this will send him running for the hills. Or at least have him telling me to just go to college so he can forget about me and move on to the next lady that is most likely lined up waiting for him. There is no way this will go well, but it needs to happen. I don't want to waste his time and I'm sure he'd appreciate that.

Max, Ashton, and Korey stand up to go and get more drinks while Lily, Janet, Kasey, and I stay at the table. The girls are going off about some annoying video they saw online that seems to be causing an issue across the world wide web. Kasey is studying my face, making it obvious he can feel my avoidant aura.

"What's wrong, baby?" He whispers to me, avoiding the nosey ears of the girls sitting across from us.

I try to avoid his question at first, "Are you excited to be almost done with school?" I ask him, a shitty attempt at best.

"Brooke." He says with a sternness and rumble that sends a lightning strike through my body, both tense and desire. "What's wrong?" He presses.

"Can we go somewhere else?" I say quietly, sending his disliked-unsureness over the edge. He stands quickly and grabs my hand gently, an interesting blend of emotions.

"We'll be right back, hold down the fort." I smile at Janet, who knows the look on my face, and Lily, who seems confused but accepts as she dives back into conversation.

He guides me to the middle of the parking lot with a hand on the small of my back, something that usually makes me feel melted to him is now making me worried. There is a sense of urgency that isn't sexual associated with the strides we are taking to a section of the lot that isn't crowded or too close to the building to be heard by anyone. A sense of urge that is new to me.

It's not quite dark outside, but it's not bright out either. Getting to that time where you can't decide if you need headlights while driving in order to see the road. We stop and he finally turns to me.

"What's going on, B?" He asks me, I can smell an angry tone as well as a whirl of concern as he speaks.

This is it. I have to do this. It's the right thing. I have to give him an out before I ruin everything all at once. I avoid his eyes and take a breath.

"When I was *missing*," I put air quotes up and he doesn't change his expression, "I did something that wasn't good." I slowly begin to explain. His fist tightens at his side.

"Who?" He asks, his cheeks turning a shade of red I hadn't seen before.

"*Who?*" I return.

"Who did you *accidentally* sleep with?" He mimics the air quotes and stands a foot farther from me than I'd like, keeping his body heat to himself, not sharing any with me.

"No one. It has nothing to do with anything like that." I counter, not being able to decide if I was angry at him for assuming I would do that or sad for him that he has dealt with a cheater in the past. I wrap my arms around my stomach, not ready to drop this news to him.

"When I was missing, I drank a lot." I pause, gauging his facial expression, no change. I continue, "Some days I drank more than half a bottle. I was really struggling." I know that's not an excuse, but it's still a fact.

"One night, I ran out and needed more. I didn't want to walk in case I ran into someone and was forced to explain myself when I wasn't ready. So I drove instead."

There is the expression change I was waiting for. His eyes turned soft but still red with anger, fists still tight with fury. At least now he saw where this was going.

"You didn't." He says to me, taking another step back.

I reach my arm out to him, hoping he will let me back in. He doesn't and I drop my hand back to my side.

"I was on my way home from the liquor store and all of a sudden my car was up on a curb and kissing a tree." I pause, giving him time.

"No one was hurt. My car is hardly damaged. I was immediately sobered up and went the fuck home. I couldn't believe what I had done. I could have hurt someone or hit someone's car or..."

He cuts me off, "Or turned out like Charlotte." Defeated, he lets out a sigh before taking a breath and speaking more. "You could have killed someone or *yourself,* Brooke. What the fuck were you thinking?" His voice is louder now, angrier. He turns away from me. "I don't know what to say. That was really fucking stupid."

"I know." A tear starts at the edge of my eye and I blink it away, hoping he doesn't see it before facing me again.

"That was *really* fucking stupid." He repeats, turning away from me a final time. He starts walking to the edge of the parking lot and turns the corner headed home without looking back a single time. The tears were uncontrollable now.

I guess I *did* ruin everything all at once.

Chapter Thirty Six

I can't fucking believe her. I can't believe what I'm hearing. She could have totaled her car, flipped and ended in a ditch, fallen asleep at the wheel. Any number of things could have happened because of her stupid decision.

"That was *really* fucking stupid." I spat out, unable to say anything else without knowing I would regret it. I walk away and refuse to look back. If I did, I might say more that I wouldn't be able to recover from. I was too angry to think properly. I needed time to let off my steam before I even thought about talking to her.

I walk inside the house, slamming the front door as I do it. Arlo startles on the couch.

"What the fuck is up with you?" He taunts. Not purposefully but I know he doesn't care to genuinely know.

"Fuck off." I mumble in his direction and leap up the stairs two at a time. My skin feels hot and my eyes are blurred. She could have fucking killed herself. What would I do then?

I throw on running clothes and sneakers and slide out the front door with the same door slam I had when I arrived.

It feels like I have been running for hours by the time I stop. My feet ached and my legs wobbled, begging to stop. But my brain couldn't let me when I wanted to. I kept running, almost double my normal amount. Too many thoughts spinning in my head for me to stop and not punch a hole in a wall. Now that I was physically too tired to assault an inanimate object, I receded into my home.

```
Workout Complete!
Summary:
7.6 miles
68 minutes
Average HR: 160 BPM
```

I landed on my bed with enough force to rattle the floor it sat on. Too tired to fight, too tired to drink water, too tired to shower, I laid there for a while. Begging myself to get up so I don't fall asleep and wither away on this unmade bed. Finally, life started creeping back into my body. My brain had been shut off for most of the time I'd been home and I was successfully avoiding feelings.When my phone rang, I sat up. Glancing at the screen I saw Ashton's name typed across it, ignoring it I forced myself off the bed and into the kitchen for beer.

Grabbing a six pack of beer I bought the other day, I see Arlo still sitting on the couch.

"What's got your panties in a twist?" He yells over to me while I crack open the first beer.

"None of your fucking business." I snarl back.

"Ah, so Brooke and you are done?" He chuckles and stands, walking in my direction. "I guess it's my turn." He says behind his teeth.

Fuck I wanted to knock every single one of them out of his stupid fucking head. Give him a fat emergency room bill.

"No, Arlo. Just fuck off."

"Well, more for me I guess." He smiles at me, "Maybe I'll transfer to her school just so I can fuck her. Send you some pictures for proof. She's just another bitch I can sleep with." He laughs menacingly.

My hands go tight at my sides, nearly cracking the beer bottle with the force of it.

This was a predicament. I need to get my head out of my ass. People make mistakes, and thankfully, this one wasn't a life-ending mistake. Yes it was stupid, but I couldn't throw away the feels I have for Brooke over something like this. This just showed that she needed some help, she needed someone to be there to show her love and care and kindness. Someone she knows will be there for her through it all. I need to get my head out of my ass.

"If only girls would fuck you sober." I throw back at him. Grabbing the rest of my pack and ascending my stairs as fast as I could.

I climb into the shower. The hot water drenches my hair and instead of further washing out my thoughts like I had hoped, it allowed them to creep back in.

I step out of the bathroom and throw on clothes. My laptop pings and I check my email, a notice from the school that classes are starting soon, as well as a list from each professor that had textbooks listed as 'Required' even though I probably wouldn't use half of them. I get lost in my thoughts staring at the screen. Different thoughts than those about Brooke.

My dad came home from work while I was sitting at the dining room table trying to work through the frustrated tears in my eyes from my math homework. Mom was in her room, door locked, snoring like usual. Dad walked into the kitchen and grabbed a beer from the fridge, not speaking to me before walking out the back slider and to the shed in the corner of the yard. That's where he spent most of his time after work and I had never been inside. Invited or sneakily.

I knock on my mom's door, calling out that I'm hungry. All I get in return is a mumble and the sound of something getting knocked off her night table. I groan and walk back to the kitchen.

We lived in a small house, barely two bedrooms and only one bathroom we had to share. The kitchen was a mere ten steps from both my parents' room and mine, sitting smack dab in the middle of the double-wide trailer.

Dinner tonight would once again consist of Cheerios and a glass of water. The only thing I really ate if I'm honest. And it was fine by me because I didn't have to bother my dad in the shed or my mom behind the locked door.

I put my bowl in the sink and strolled off to my room, avoiding any more tear jerking homework.

My phone rings again, I answer the phone hastily.

"What?" I say to the receiver.

"Are you okay?" Max questions, I can hear the background music at Blazer's and the slur of his words. Brooke must not have said anything to them. Good girl.

"Fine. Why?" Short and to the point.

"You left us. Drinking without you. What's going on?" I can practically see his bloodshot eyes, glossed with sadness that I ruined our last summer outing.

"I had to take care of something. Is Brooke there?" I reply.

"Yeah she is, she's had a few more drinks though…" I hear the slight concern in his voice. *Fuck.* I need to go get her before she does something even more stupid. I look to my desk and see the empty cardboard that once housed a six pack of beer and next to it see the other five empty bottles on the ground. *Fuck.* I couldn't go get her.

"Can you make sure she gets home okay? I'll check in with her later." I try to hide my upset and the warmth I can feel from the alcohol setting in.

"Yeah man, youuuu got it!" He says before ending the call. But he didn't end it before I heard Brooke asking for food. The sound of her drunken voice lit up something inside of me. I couldn't quite put my finger on it, but I knew I didn't want that to be the last time I heard her voice.

Chapter Thirty Seven

I grab my suitcase from the closet. I come home from school pretty often since it's only two hours away so I only pack clothes and hygiene essentials, really. I've got everything else I need at my dorm. Luckily, they keep an eye on things when we go home for breaks and I have scholarships (pity money, but free money nonetheless) to pay for my housing so I don't have to worry about wasted money.

I pack all the clothes and zip my suitcase, standing it up in the corner of my room to serve as a constant reminder of the shit storm to come. My second bag holds all my bathroom-like things. Curling iron, straightening iron, makeup bag, toothbrush, shampoo, conditioner, body wash, all those things.

I take the sheets off my bed and pillowcases off the pillows, starting them in the washing machine and walking into the kitchen. I pull out a bowl and spoon, and pour in some cereal and milk. I sit at the table and start to eat when Beverly comes in the kitchen and mimics my breakfast.

"You all packed up?" She asks, sitting across from me.

"Sadly, yes." I sigh.

"You won't be gone too long, and you're always welcome to come for a weekend whenever you want." She says to me, I know she's truthful. She loves when I pay her a surprise visit.

"Yeah but it still sucks having to leave in the first place. I wish I could have just done online school." I say before taking my last bite of cereal and standing to load my dishes in the dishwasher.

"I know, but this way you have most of your tuition paid." She says back to me, still enjoying her simple breakfast.

"That's true. The scholarships were a life saver." I started the coffee pot, mostly for her. I know she'll want more.

The dryer buzzes and I grab my sheets, making my bed for the last time before I leave. It's still relatively early in the morning and I have a while before I need to hit the road. My plan is to smoke myself into comfortable oblivion, shower, and nap if my body wants to. It's the last day of summer and I need to spend it well.

I wasn't surprised by Kasey's reaction to my news. I mean, I was and I wasn't. I knew he would be upset but I didn't think he would storm off. Never to be heard from again. He didn't text me to make sure I had gotten home. Max had tried to call him when I snuck off to the bathroom a little while after I gave a half-assed lie that he had to run home for something.

Standing at my window, I blow my last hit from the joint out into the fresh air and put the roach into my box with the lighter. I grab my bluetooth speaker and walk into my bathroom. Turning on some acoustic chill playlist that's premade for people wanting to relax, I climb into the hot water falling from the spout. I wash my hair first, condition, and then wash my body. When I step out, I get the sudden urge to sleep. Just my plan.

I put on an oversized T-shirt and a pair of underwear. The perfect attire for a mid-morning nap. I slump into bed, the music still playing, and drift off into dreamland.

My dream takes me back to my first date with Kasey. How perfectly it went. The boardwalk, dinner, spontaneous swimming. It was a dream come true, and now I'm reliving it. The feeling I had in my stomach when he put his hand in the small of my back. The way he kissed me in the water, his lips salty of the ocean and soft like nothing I've felt before. They way his hands wrap around mine.

We have gotten so close over the last couple of months and I am so grateful. He is everything I have ever wanted in a person. A person to call mine. I don't want to fuck it up by going back to school. Or by making him hate me over my drunken mistake.

What if I come back and he doesn't me? Or he finds someone better than me? Or he was never really that serious about me in the first place? Or this night of regret pries us apart forever? What if he can't ever look at me the same because I could have killed someone or myself?

Stop it, Brooke. It's not a joke. It's not your heart playing tricks on you. It's not some evil revenge plan from Don. It's happiness. It's something you're not used to so when it happens you try to push it away. You try to sabotage it. You ruin it before it ruins you. This is not something you need to ruin. So you need to try and fix it before it's too late.

I wake up and check the time on my phone. It's still only two o'clock, I'm not getting on the road until five or six because traffic won't be too bad and when I get there it'll give me just enough time to unpack and climb into bed for the first day of classes the next day. What an exciting time.

I can hear my aunt in the kitchen, doing dishes from the dinner she hosted for all my friends last night. The original group sat around the table laughing and trading stories and letting Beverly hear all of the crazy and fun things we were up to this summer. It was a really fun time, especially to include her in that portion of my life more than before. I think she needed that. She needed to feel like part of a community outside of work.

I already said my goodbyes to my friends. They were tear jerking and uncomfortably sad. I can understand a little of why though. Goodbyes are difficult. They always are. Unless you don't care if you never see that person again. Like the clerk at the gas station or the grocery store. But when it comes to the people you care about, those ones are difficult.

I hadn't said goodbye to Kasey. I haven't heard from him since he stormed off. The way that conversation ended left a pit in my gut and I didn't like it.

I don't want to get out of bed yet. So I don't. I doom scroll for an hour or so until there's a knock at the front door and I hear Beverly shout "Can you get that?"

I groan and sit up out of bed, not bothering to put shorts on because the shirt is long enough to cover me up.

Chapter Thirty Eight

My phone blares in my ear. I didn't plug it in last night so it sits annoyingly close to my pillow. Emitting a disgusting alarm from the speaker and I rub my hand across the sheets in desperate search of it. Finally I click the side button and turn it off.

Today is the day Brooke is leaving. I have come to my senses about the drunken incident and know that she's not the kind of person to do that on the regular and continue to disappoint me like my mother would. I'm not happy with the way I stormed off instead of a proper goodbye at the least. I need more. I need her to know that I love her. I need her to know I am here.

I slide out of bed and walk to my shower, turning the water to a scorching level of hot, and climb in with no regrets. I scrub my body with soap and run my hands through my hair to make sure I got all the shampoo out. When I get out, I dry out my hair and wrap the towel around my body. I pick clothes that will show I care and that I'm trying and that I'm not perfect.

Black jeans, a nice blue T-shirt that matches my eyes with a single pocket on the left chest, and my white shoes. I walk down the first flight of stairs and see Arlo sitting on the couch, sloppily eating a bagel. He must be very hungover.

"You're lucky she leaves today, buddy." He says to me in the kitchen, grinning mischievously.

"Fuck you." I say back with no emotion in my voice. Making it more matter-of-fact than inviting further commentary. He takes the hint for once and ignores me. He doesn't deserve to know how beautiful she is on the inside, or how her lips part slightly when she sleeps, or how she likes to sleep in a cold room with a big blanket and hates hot ones. I pour myself a cup of coffee and drink it quickly, wanting to get away from his presence as soon as I can. Walking down the second flight of stairs and out the front door.

On the way to Brooke's, I stop at the grocery store and buy her a bouquet of flowers. They really sold me with the deep green wrapping paper they bunched around the pink and purple daisies, finishing the look with a piece of twine keeping at all together.

I park my car on the street and take a few breaths before I turn the engine off and get out. I walk up the driveway and stop at her door. Taking another breath before knocking on it. I hear Beverly shout and a few moments later the door swings open.

She is gorgeous. Long shirt and messy hair. No makeup and sleep written across her face. She is *gorgeous*.

"Hey." She says, timid but I can see her excitement and shock that I'm here. She eyes the bouquet of flowers in my hand.

"Hey, Brooke." I say and look her up and down, "Can I come in for a few?" Handing her the flowers.

She looks over her shoulder at Beverly who is now watching us smiling. "Yeah, sure." Brooke says, now shyly smiling as well and takes the flowers from my hands.

I take my shoes off inside the front door, set them to the side, and say hello to Beverly as Brooke hands her the bouquet, and follow Brooke to her room. Beverly shouts out to us, "I'm gonna run to the store! Need anything?"

"No thank you!" Brooke responds as we walk in her room. She turns to me, I can see she is confused and I know she thinks I came over to yell at her more, but I'm hoping the scent of fresh flowers showed her that wasn't my intention. "Everything okay?"

The moment her door closes I grab her waist and spin her so her back is towards the wall and slowly walk towards it to press her against it gently. Her breath hitches. I look her in the eyes for a moment, knowing I need to savor this moment but I can't wait any longer. My lips crash into her, they grow a mind of their own.

Kissing her makes all my worries dissipate in a matter of moments. I am no longer afraid of what's to come. I now have the confidence to say what I need to. And I need to say it before that confidence disappears.

I pull away from her and grab her hand, leading her to the bed where we lay down next to each other, her head on my chest where it belongs. Our hands dance with each other in the air. This is such a peaceful moment you could photograph it and put it in a lovey-dovey couples magazine for wedding or honeymoon venues. As cheesy as it looks, it feels so *fucking* good.

Even the non-sexual intimate moments with her make sparks fly throughout my body. Our silly conversations and our laughs and our stories and our arguments. It all makes my heart burst in happiness because at least I get to experience it with her.

"Brooke." I start, "What you did was really dumb. I hope you know my anger is fear. Fear that I could have lost you. Fear that I could have had to go on without you. I can't imagine that." I can't slow down, "Can I wait for you? I guess that's not a fair ask because you'll have to wait for me since you'll be done with school sooner but I just can't imagine living my life without you and I don't want to lose you. I have grown so close to you and grown so much within myself since we reconnected and it's been the most beautiful thing to me."

"I understand if you don't feel the same way but I just need to get all this off my chest before you leave because I want to be able to say I gave it an honest shot and that I am not mad at *you* for what happened I was just scared." I take a big breath. That must be a lot to process. I spoke faster than I was planning to.

"There are a lot of things that I feel like I need in this life. And a lot of things that I feel like I could live without. And I haven't figured all of that out yet because life is crazy and you never really know what you need or don't need until it happens. But something I know for sure I need is a future with you."

"Kasey…" She says after a moment. My heart races and I start to feel overheated and sweaty. Scared of what she's going to say next. Her hand rests on my chest as she snuggles closer to me.

"You have become so important to me. I can't imagine living my life without you either." She finally says. "I'm sorry for being dumb. I'm not usually like that." Her hand reaches for mine and our fingers interlace. I can sense her anxiety and she is taking it out on my hands instead of her rings, which she doesn't have on, or her bouncing leg.

I've noticed and learned so much about Brooke in the last few months. I am mad at myself that it took this long to really start to understand her. But I am happier than ever that we finally connected in the way I wanted to all along. I want her in my life for as long as I am living. Coming home to Brooke everyday, or her coming home to me, would truly be the most precious thing I could ask for in this world.

Sparks fly when I touch her. My stomach flips when she looks at me. I really haven't ever felt a connection like this, ever. I don't want to lose it or waste it on the difficulties life can bring. I need to fight for this. I need to show her how badly I want her. I need to find a way to make this work.

I think she is all I need in life. It wouldn't heal my issues, but it sure would make tackling them a hell of a lot better. Knowing she loves and supports me back is enough for me to feel like I am on top of the world.

My nerves settle a little. I know what else I need to say, and I think she will reciprocate it. I feel good. Confident. Strong.

"I love you, Brooke." I say after a few moments of silence. I can feel her holding her breath. She sits up and turns to look at me. I can't help but notice her natural beauty. Her eyes that could stop a storm from hitting the streets. A smile that can light an entire island. Hair that can wrap around your soul and hold you close. A body that will have you stopped in your tracks.

"I love you, Kasey."